Von Mozan

Dirty Dog

Jewelled Books

Copyright © 2006 & 2022 by Nicholas Levi Harrison

The right of Nicholas Levi Harrison P/K/A Von Mozar to be identified as the Author of the Work has been asserted by him in accordance with the Copyright, Designs and Patents Act 1988.

First published in Great Britain as Sexfiend in 2006
by WATERBUCK PUBLISHING LIMITED

Published as Dirty Dog in 2022
by JEWELLED BOOKS

Conditions:

All rights reserved.

No part of this publication may be reproduced, stored in a retrieval system, or transmitted, in any form or by any means without the prior written permission of the publisher, nor be otherwise circulated in any form of binding or cover other than that in which it is published and without a similar condition being imposed on the subsequent purchaser.

All characters in this publication are fictitious and any resemblance to real persons, living or dead,
is purely coincidental.

Dear reader,

I greatly appreciate you purchasing my book, and I hope you enjoy it as much as I enjoyed writing it.

Once you finish reading the book, if you don't mind, I would love to get your feedback.

Please leave a review at Amazon.

Dirty Dog

Prologue

Rundown Housing Estate

Chapter i

THE LARGE DOUBLE ROOM is quiet and filled with seven sleeping bodies. Eschewal, twelve years old, lays on a bed with his auntie, who is four years his senior, along with his baby brother and sister. The bed opposite occupies his three older brothers.

The nudging signal comes to him. He knows what it means, tries to ignore it, but she will not let him. Her hot breath blows down his left ear as she speaks, "Oi, you wanna do it?" she says in a whisper.

He wants to tell her no, but she persists with her ample thighs. "Oi, Eros, are you sleeping?"

He pretends he is and lets out a moan, but she continues, "Hey, Eros, do you want to do it?"

He answers in a groggy voice, "Mmmm, what did you say?"

"Do you want to do it?" she replies.

With disbelief, he says, "What... now?"

"Yeah, come on, man, please..."

The feeling of butterflies swirls in his stomach, and as if it causes him extreme pain to move, he climbs on top and meets with his auntie's half-naked body.

She pulls down his underpants and then guides his penis into her vagina.

He places his head on her firm young breasts and bounces his body up and down.

Her hot breath blows down his right ear as she moans and grunts.

He buries his face in the mattress as the sex becomes

more intense. The following experience is new to him but not so unique that he did not know it was coming. His butt cheeks clench as he ejaculates.

They carry on pumping for a while longer. She squeals for a moment or two, then before he can slip off, she pushes him off.

He rolls onto his back, then onto his front as he attempts to stifle that sickening feeling he always gets after having sex with his aunt. It runs through his bones and makes him feel sinful, filthy, and evil. At this moment, he wishes he could rip his insides out and become another person, no longer living in poverty and experiencing horrors.

He wants to cry but holds the tears because the worst thing about the experience is that it makes him feel beautiful inside when it begins and before it ends. And this beauty is stronger than the sickening after effects.

He finally closes his eyes, hoping this haunting was another one of those dreams.

Eight Years Later

Chapter ii

ESCHEWAL TOSSES AND TURNS then shoots open his eyes. Sweat streams down his face as his heart races. He grabs his penis, which is rock hard, then realizes the haunting is one of those neurotic dreams he has from time to time.

He panics as he finds himself handcuffed to a hospital bed. Earlier, a car knocked him down as he tried to escape the police.

He looks to his left, and two other beds come into view. The one in the middle is empty, but its sheets are ruffled. The one at the end is neatly made up. He looks towards the ceiling and closes his eyes.

He has had enough of the street life and of being chased by the police. He has had enough of being locked up in cells, and most of all, he has had enough of feeling pain. Tears come to his eyes as nothing comes to his mind on how to escape the street life that he has been trapped in since the days he started having sex with his aunt.

He whispers to himself, "Why?" Before he can repeat, why me? A flood of tears from his repressed pain, anger, and ignorance roll down his face.

As he bawls, he loses himself and slips into his private world, and all past and present sounds are blocked out. While there, he wishes someone could show him how to find happiness. All he wants is to lead a good life that involves marriage, children, and a job.

Von Mozan

Gently in the background, the sound of music and a powerful light voice shakes Eschewal out of his semi-consciousness. "Do you want me to call someone, son?" repeats the voice.

Eschewal opens his eyes but does not answer.

The voice continues questioning, "What are all those tears for?"

Eschewal remains silent.

The voice continues, "I bet I can guess why you're crying. You wish you could have the nice things in life without experiencing any pain."

That sentence gets Eschewal's full attention. He wipes his tears and focuses on the old man's wrinkled face and strong, youthful eyes, which reflect genuine honesty.

The old man stares at Eschewal before continuing, "What if I told you that the words in this book," the old man removes a black book from under his pillow, "hold the key to making you happy, rich, and powerful enough never again to feel pain. Would you believe me?"

Eschewal says, "I don't know, does it?"

"Yes, it does, and much more, just as long as you read it and use the knowledge. But remember, whatever you learn, you do not need to believe; you need to accept."

Eschewal chuckles. He holds his waist, and as he sits up, his face grimaces from the pain. "Listen, I don't read books," he says.

The old man nods. "I know you don't read. Most people where you come from don't either. That's why most experience a life of pain and hardship." The old man rises slightly from the bed and extends the black book towards Eschewal. "Take it, read the book."

Eschewal does not take the black book, but he is intrigued and says, "But why give me the book?"

Dirty Dog

The old man smiles and says, "I have finished with it; I no longer need it."

Eschewal extends his hand but is restricted by the handcuffs.

The old man stretches closer and says, "Remember, the use of knowledge is power…" then drops the black book into Eschewal's hand.

The old man continues talking, but, as if told to focus and read the letters on the board by an optician, Eschewal is captivated by the black book's title:

HOW TO CREATE YOUR DESTINY AND FOREVER LIVE LIFE WITH HAPPINESS & RICHES!

Eschewal looks up towards the old man for an explanation of the title, but the old man has already left the room. This leaves him without a choice. He opens the black book.

Chapter iii

*E*SCHEWAL READS THE FIRST line of the black book: *You're the creator of your destiny.* Surprise dons his face. He licks his lips and continues reading.

For over 2000 years, destructive governments have blocked the immense power within every human mind.

He removes his eyes from the page and blinks towards the ceiling. He wonders what could be this immense power. His heart pounds inside his chest. He takes a deep breath and continues reading.

That immense power consists of entirely using one's volitional conceptual consciousness. What is volitional conceptual consciousness? It is the ability to debate with oneself, make decisions, and ultimately create new values. One can only create new values after one has learned how to unleash one's full volitional conceptual consciousness.

He places the black book on his chest and closes his eyes. He knows the next thing the black book will tell him is how to unleash his full volitional conceptual consciousness, so he opens his eyes and continues reading.

To unleash one's full volitional conceptual consciousness, one must disconnect from the destructive matrix of corrupt forces by rejecting anything that destroys the human organism, whether the threat is mental or physical. The following are the most common.

In a slow, careful manner, he reads aloud the list of items he must disconnect from: *Sugar, Alcohol, Caffeine, Tobacco, Narcotics, Promiscuity, Objective Crime,*

Von Mozan

Gambling, Destructive Governments, Mysticism, Religion and Cults.

The black book continues: *Once disconnected from those destructive forces, one will unleash the full power of one's volitional conceptual consciousness. This will give one the ability to become a creator of values. Then, automatically, happiness & riches will flow to one.*

A feeling of excitement seeps through him as he is promised happiness & riches. He smiles because he dreams of happiness and enough money to leave the street life all his life. Therefore, the decision to believe what the black book promises is an easy one.

He lays the black book on his chest and plans to disconnect from the list of destructive forces.

Part One
Five Years Later

Chapter 1

*E*SCHEWAL SITS AT HIS desk in a shirt and tie, staring at his computer screen. It has taken a while, but he has disconnected from all the destructive forces. The last destructive force, which he disconnected from, was promiscuous sex. This was the hardest because he had always conflicted with the animal in man – *The Dog*.

The Dog had made him do terrible things in the past and always made him feel sick and twisted afterward. So when he had learned what promiscuity meant, he was glad he had to "fight" *The Dog* and get rid of it to become a creator of values and receive the happiness & riches the black book promised.

Two years after "killing" *The Dog*, he is now waiting to become a creator of values, but unfortunately, he has not clearly understood the second requirement in achieving this. He had thought by just reading the black book and disconnecting from all the destructive forces; he would automatically become a creator of values and receive happiness & riches. But this has not happened, and he is wondering *why?*

He thinks back to that night he laid in the hospital bed. He did not sleep until he finished reading the black book, which drew him from that very first page to a world outside himself.

As he read more of the black book, he was hit by words he had never seen before. They were strange words, but within sentences amongst other common

Dirty Dog

words, he had just about understood the message and the power of the black book. Once he reached the end, he was warned:

Be careful to whom you expose this knowledge. Many will become angry (even though they implicitly know the reality) and quickly defend the destructive matrix of corrupt forces with a hundred different rationalizations. These people do not want to be disconnected because the corrupt forces provide short-term happiness (which leads to long-term problems). Remember: most people are willing to trade their health and life in exchange for destructive stimulation.

He smiles and shuts down his computer. He has to admit that since the moment he decided to disconnect from the destructive forces, his life has been much better. He shakes his head at still not understanding why he has not yet become a creator of values.

He rises from his desk, unaware that the answer to his question will soon reveal itself, but not before taking him to the dark depths of his soul.

Chapter 2

AT FIVE TO SIX, Eschewal has already left the building. As he steps outside, the cool fresh air hits him and seems to shake off the oppressive stress of the office. He beams a cheesy grin because he has a definite date for later on. Her name is Keneisha. He had met her four months ago. He had taken her out on two expensive dates without getting as much as a kiss. This did not matter because she had promised him he would get lucky at the weekend. This promise had gotten him through his grueling working week.

A wider smile dons his face as he pads past a row of shopfronts. His phone rings; it is Keneisha. He pumps his fist out of joy as he hopes she is calling to tell him to pick her up earlier.

He answers the phone with his calm, steady, sexy voice, "Yeah, what's up, Keneisha?"

Her voice drops a tone, and she says, "Oh babes, I'm so sorry, I can't make it again."

For a second, he loses his voice as hot heat rises inside of him. Her words feel like the impact of a car crash, resulting in his whole world collapsing. A lump appears in his throat, but he controls his voice and replies, "Yeah, why, though?"

"Oh, at the last minute, I've been asked to babysit my goddaughter. You understand, don't you?"

He replies yes, which is a lie because he does not understand. *'How could she do me like this?'* he thinks.

She ends the call with the promise that she will meet

him tomorrow, another lie. She has a better date for later on and tomorrow, so her "goddaughter" is really Godfrey, a big-time drug dealer with a mansion in the countryside.

From across the street, someone hollers Eschewal's pet name (which everyone calls him, except loved ones and the police).

"Oi, Eros, you listening?"

"Oh shit, it's Tek," says Eschewal to himself.

Back in the day, Tek was always thinking up new ways to make illegal money, but his ideas always seemed to get Eschewal arrested whenever he decided to hustle with Tek.

Tek calls again.

"Ah, what the hell does he want, man? I bet he wants to ask if I'm down with one of his bait moves," a scowl develops on Eschewal's face, *"'but I'm sure he knows I don't make money on the road anymore?"* He sucks his teeth and continues thinking, *"It's taken me five years to break away from the road, so why does this waste-man wanna drag me back down?"* He raises one finger in the air and shouts back at Tek, "Just cool, man, I'm in a rush. Are you still on the same number?"

Tek nods.

"Alright, man, I'll ding you little more from now."

Tek raises his right hand in the air.

Eschewal nods; he raises his fist, then turns down the first road on his right with no intention of ever phoning Tek.

Chapter 3

ESCHEWAL'S MIND SPINS. HE feels like calling Keneisha back and begging her to meet him when his pet name is again hollered. This time from the top of a bedroom window. He looks up and spots another thug he grew up with on the mean streets. Deuce is a natural fighter with huge muscles, medium in height with a face that is a bit too pretty for a man.

Eschewal's heart pounds inside his chest. He cannot remember the reason why he and Deuce stopped hanging out; it might have been over an argument that could now lead to a fight. He licks his lips and controls his voice, trying not to show his fear. "Yeah, what's going on, bro?"

"Boy, nothing, cuz. Oi, wait there. I'm gonna come down and rap to you."

At that moment, Eschewal's legs shake. He feels as if 20 kilos of weight has been attached to his wrist. His mind tells his legs to run, but his legs do not respond. His male pride kicks in. He tells himself, *"Come on, bruv, don't be a punk."* He shakes his head and wonders, *'What happened to that killer instinct? Has that black book turned me into a pussy?'*

He thinks hard about those thoughts and then realizes that the black book has not only made him value his own life; it has made him value the lives of others also. His thoughts break as the front door opens.

Deuce comes charging out.

Von Mozan

Eschewal holds his breath, waiting to block the impact from a punch.

Deuce's arms extend towards Eschewal and embrace him with a handshake and a hug. "What's up, blood? I ain't seen you for long, cuz. What's going on, man? What's popping? What's good?"

Eschewal pulls back and looks square into Deuce's eyes, wanting to see if he is for real. He cannot tell, so he plays along. "Just chilling, bruv, man's working now, you get me?"

Deuce releases his grip on Eschewal and replies, "Yeah? Man's working too, fam. You feel me? I left the grime. Road is too sticky. It's a long ting."

Eschewal smiles as he relaxes. "Course, course, cuz, the streets are long, blood, you done know. So, where are you working now anyway?"

Deuce sucks his teeth and then answers, "I sell phones, blood. Trust me, it's all right, blood. You know how much chicks man's slapped from the time I've been selling phones."

"Yeah, true stories?" says Eschewal, as he grows a broad smile, remembering that Deuce had always been known as a player and would have many girlfriends at the same time.

"Yeah, bruv, one's coming down right now, bruv. I sold her a heavy phone and gave her a good deal. You feel me, player? Course." Deuce rubs his chin. He points at Eschewal. "Oi, you know what, though, bruv? This ting is a little freak, cuz. Man can battery it, standard."

Eschewal's eyes widen as he remembers taking turns to have sex with girls back in the day. He hated doing it because he never liked having unemotional sex. It always made him feel dirty afterward, and not only that, there was always a chance that the girl would call rape.

Dirty Dog

He looks Deuce in his eyes and wants to say no, but the whole week of anticipating some good sex has woken *The Dog* in him. He feels as if blood from his brain is flowing down to his penis, making him light-headed. "Yeah, true stories, yeah, she's up for battery?" He asks as he leans his elbow on the front gate.

"Course, bruv, I'm not gonna lie to you." Deuce opens his front door and invites Eschewal inside.

Eschewal steps into the house saying, "Yeah, man, I'm down," with words from the black book racing through his mind: *Promiscuous sex lowers one's self-esteem through short-term happiness, ultimately leading to long-term problems.*

Chapter 4

AS THE DOOR CLOSES behind Eschewal, Deuce's phone rings. "Yeah, hello," he says, then pokes Eschewal's shoulder to get his attention. Eschewal looks at him. Deuce pulls the phone away from his mouth and whispers to Eschewal, "It's her, blood." Deuce puts the phone back to his ear. "Yeah, yeah, babes," he continues, "take the first right, then the second left, and you'll be on my road. Come to 108… yeah, alright." He ends the call and then squeals, "Rudeboy, she's round the corner, blood!" He pushes open a door and tells Eschewal to follow.

He leads Eschewal into a large room that contains a long sofa, a table, and green and brown paisley wallpaper. "Yeah, blood. You listening? This is how we're gonna run it. When she comes, yeah, you wait in here and don't make her see you. I'll bring her straight to my room and go thru, then tell her I'm gonna take a piss. That's when you go in and kill it."

Eschewal thinks for a second, then says, "Nah, bro, that don't sound like no battery. That's a long ting."

Deuce shuts his eyes, then opens them and shrugs. "How? It's not long. What's wrong with you, man? Listen, this chick is dumb, and the room is gonna be dark, so when you go in, just act like you're me, innit."

Eschewal pauses in thought, but Deuce's phone rings before he can run through the possible consequences of his actions.

Von Mozan

    Deuce answers. The girl is outside. He clicks off his phone and then says, "So what you saying?" Before Eschewal can answer, Deuce adds, "You're down, man, just cool," then leaves the room.

    Eschewal runs to the window and peeps through the curtain. Subconsciously he licks his lips as he sees the girl walking towards the door. His penis grows hard. His eyes glaze over as *The Dog's* imaginary growl makes him lust after the girl's firm young body. Images of him having sex with her flood his mind, and at that moment, he knows *The Dog* has won, and all the wrong he is about to do is pushed aside.

Chapter 5

BEFORE ESCHEWAL KNOWS IT, he stands in the dark room, looking over at the girl. She says, "Oi, babes, you took long in the bathroom, man."
His heart skips a beat. He pushes his chest out before he answers, and with the best impersonation of Deuce, he says, "Just cool, man. What you ready for the second round?"

The girl wriggles her body on the bed and says, "What do you think?"

He smiles and steps forward. "Alright then, turn around."

The girl rises to her knees and turns her backside towards him. His heart pounds in his chest, and his stomach feels as if it is being tied in knots. He cannot believe that it is working. He calms himself and then rubs his hand over her backside. "Oh flip, you're so sexy."

The girl stops wriggling and looks over her shoulder as if the words he had used are not words Deuce would have used. Before she can take any other action, Eschewal sticks his fingers into her vagina. She moans and grips the sheets.

Adrenalin runs through him, and he thinks, *'I need to put it in quick enough so she won't pull away and get a better look at my face.'* With his free hand, he unzips his jeans. His penis jumps out. He dips into his back pocket, slips out a condom, bites it open, and then rolls it on. He then positions his penis towards the

Von Mozan

girl's vagina, and in one swift movement, he removes his fingers and then penetrates.

The girl shoots forward. He grabs her waist and pulls her back. Then faster and faster, he slides in and out. The girl moans and crawls forward. By now, he is in his own world, trying to ejaculate as quickly as possible.

He opens his eyes and realizes the girl has reached the curtain and is pulling it open to let in the evening sun so that she can see his face.

He falls forward onto her. He shakes a little as if he is ejaculating.

The girl lets go of the curtain.

He slides out his penis, then says, "Yeah, babes, I've cum."

The girl springs around towards him, but all she sees is the back of his shadow leaving the room.

Chapter 6

OUTSIDE THE ROOM, DEUCE had been masturbating as he listened to Eschewal having sex. He ejaculated in his left palm and is now in the bathroom washing his hands.

Eschewal stands in the hallway, not knowing where to go. As his mind races, he wipes his sweaty hands down his trousers and hopes the girl does not burst out of the bedroom.

The bathroom door opens, and Deuce peeps out. "Oi, Eros, come," he says.

Eschewal puts his hands into his pockets and walks into the bathroom.

Deuce closes the door. "Yes, blood, I heard you killing it, cuz."

Eschewal jumps into his player dialogue as he says with a fake laugh and a smile, "Course, course, blood, I mashed that down." Really he feels disgusted and wishes he could reverse time.

Deuce squeals. He hits fist with Eschewal.

Eschewal's eyebrows scrunch together, and the corners of his mouth turn down. "Oi, you know what, though? I think she knew it wasn't you, rudeboy. I swear down, blood she try buss the curtain on man, so I had to all sink it deeper until she let go of it, blood."

Before Deuce can respond, the girl hollers for him. He opens the bathroom door and yells, "I'm just in the bathroom. Wait there; I'm coming." He closes

Von Mozan

the door and turns to Eschewal. A cunning thought comes to him. He needs a driver to drive him to meet different girls because his girlfriend almost caught him with one of his girls in his car. "Listen, bruv, don't watch that, she's some dumb bitch. She don't know nothing, so just cool, man, everything is jiggy." He leads Eschewal out of the bathroom.

"Alright, gee."

Deuce whispers, "Oi, rudeboy, let me get your number." He pulls out his phone and lets Eschewal punch in his number. He points towards the front door. "Yeah, just creep out, yeah. I'll give you a one ding, and you'll get my number."

Eschewal nods.

Deuce again whispers, "Alright, blood, we link, yeah?" He hits fist with Eschewal once more and then steps into his bedroom. He switches on the bedroom light and says, "What's up, babes? How you screaming out my name like that? I'm a man, not a machine, you know."

The girl squints her eyes and then smirks. "Um, is there anyone else in the house, Mark, uh?" she says with suspicion.

Mark is the alias that Deuce gave the girl. He scrunches his eyebrows together. "How you mean if there's someone else in the house?" He sucks his teeth. "Nah, it's just you and me. Like, who else is meant to be here?"

The girl shakes her head and then says, "Um, no one," but within her mind, she is sure that was a different penis inside her. Nothing could tell her differently, but she will keep it to herself for one reason: the shame of being played for a fool.

Deuce rubs his chest and turns on the TV with a cunning smile. It disappears as he turns around and jumps on the bed. As he does, Eschewal turns from

Dirty Dog

listening at the bedroom door. He had to be sure that the girl was not aware, and with tremendous guilt and feeling dirty, he walks down the stairs, creeps out the front door, and onto the street.

Chapter 7

"HEY? LARGE OR SMALL?"

"Small, please," replies Eschewal to the big-boned woman behind the food counter. He gives her the payment, and without a smile, she hands over his change. He slips it into his pocket and sits on one of the soft stools the restaurant provides for takeaway customers.

As he sits, his thoughts travel back to when he was stealing sex. He shakes his head. He cannot believe his need to orgasm drove him to the thin line between sex and rape. His heart sinks, and he thinks, *'Maybe it was rape?'* his whole body turns hot. He closes his eyes and then runs through in his mind what represents rape. He reassures himself, *'I didn't force the girl; she gave it to me, but she only gave it because she thought I was Deuce. Would she have given it to me if she knew it wasn't?'* That question weighs on his mind. He looks towards his feet and shrugs off the question by telling himself, *'Yeah, man; she knew it was someone else. She just played the fool so she could get sexed by two different men.'*

That new idea of the situation makes him feel better. It makes him relax, and visions of him sinking his penis in and out of the girl's vagina flood his mind. He feels as if *The Dog* is forcing his penis to grow hard. The sexual pictures now flick through his mind a thousand paces a minute. He grabs his penis and then remembers that he did not ejaculate.

Von Mozar

The Dog seems to be howling to satisfy the need to orgasm – the assault is too overwhelming. He bites his lip. He knows *The Dog* is out of its cage. He shakes his head and says to himself, *'Damn, why did Keneisha have to blow me out and release this dirty dog in me? After all that effort I put in to get rid of it.'*

He closes his eyes and continues to reason with himself, *'Cha, I swear the black book is a joke. I've done everything it said, yet I've not become a creator of values.'*

He sucks his teeth and looks at his phone. He scrolls through the contacts. 'Flip, no girls to call.' He had deleted all the girls on his phone when he decided to disconnect from promiscuous sex.

'Ah, what am I gonna do now to release?' He laughs to himself. *'Geez, it looks like I might have to pay for a prostitute.'* He sucks his teeth. *'Nah, that's long. I can't slip like that.'* He looks over at the big-boned woman. He contemplates asking her out on a date. He tries to catch her eye as she places the lid on his food. She does not look up until the food is packed into the white plastic bag. She gives him the bag without a smile.

He says, "Thank you," and takes the bag. He turns on his heels and exits the restaurant with his mind spinning on releasing his sexual tension.

Chapter 8

*E*SCHEWAL TURNS RIGHT AS he steps out of the restaurant and walks into an off-licence to buy a sugar-free drink.

Outside of the off-licence stands a young lady by a bus stop. She looks over at him as he pays for his drink.

She had been making her way to meet a guy, but on the way, he called and said he could no longer meet her. All week she had prepared for the date; it was the one thing that got her through her stressful week at work. She had planned on having sex with the guy on the first night. She had visions of being stretched out on a bed with her legs in the air and her hair messed up from rough intercourse. Her sights are now set firmly on Eschewal. She contemplates how to get his attention. He steps out of the off-licence. Her nerves give, and she looks away just quick enough for him not to have noticed that she was staring.

He glances at her and feels she is not his usual type. She is a bit on the chunky side but relatively tall, so she carries the chunkiness well.

He steps past her and notices that her eyes twitch towards him. At that moment, it is as if something in the air flashes images of him having sex with her in his flat.

As if *The Dog* had burst out of his back and stopped him in his tracks, which makes him think, *'She's just like you; all she wants is a little sexual release. Just step to her. All she can say is no.'*

He turns around, his nerves running a rampage. He heads back to her like someone who has nothing to lose.

He gets her attention. She turns around with a broad smile like she has won the lottery.

"Sorry, what did you say?" she says.

Like a good actor, he hides his nervousness and repeats, "I said, what is a beautiful girl like you doing alone on a Friday night?"

She smiles. "Oh, I came from visiting my grandparents. I'm just on my way home."

He nods. "Yeah, so what's your name anyway?"

"Camille!"

He has already forgotten her name. He extends his hand. "Nice to meet you, babes. My name's Eros." He does not let go of her hand. "So you're saying that you're just going home?"

She nods.

"Ok, so if that's all you're doing, what would you say if I invited you around to my flat for something to eat?" He holds his breath while waiting for her reply and tries to think of something cool to say if she says no.

Slowly, her lips begin to stretch open, revealing her white teeth. It is not yet certain if her mouth is turning up into a smile until she says, "Yeah, alright."

He pauses for a moment and thinks, *'That seemed too easy. Maybe there is something wrong with this chick?'* He is sure he hears *The Dog* barking, which he interprets as *The Dog* demanding that he stop thinking. His heart skips a beat as he leads her to his home.

Chapter 9

ESCHEWAL HAS JUST FINISHED eating. He sits on his sofa. The TV is tuned to a music video channel. Camille sits to his right staring at the TV.

They have not talked much since they got in the flat, and the situation seems to be growing tense. Eschewal deliberates, *'I wonder if the only way to get sex tonight is to lick it before I can stick it?'*

He looks at her glass; the drink is almost finished. He uses this as an icebreaker. "Um, would you like another drink?"

She turns to him and smiles. "No, thank you."

He holds her stare and says, "So, babes, you don't have a boyfriend?"

She bats her eyelids. "No, not at the moment. What, have you got a girl?"

He looks towards his feet. "Nah, I ain't got a girl."

Her eyes glisten with hope; he does not notice.

He rubs his chin. "Um, babes, can I ask you something?"

She nods. "Yeah, go on."

He grins to himself. "Do you like sex?"

"Yeah, of course!" she replies with a nod.

His grin spreads wider. "What type of sex do you like?" He does not give her a chance to answer. "I bet you like oral?"

"Mmmm, yeah." Her eyes drift off as if she is imagining oral sex.

Eschewal's penis grows big and stiff; it throbs as his

heart pumps more and more blood into his erection. He leans back on the sofa and controls his eagerness. He says, "I bet you like giving it too, don't you, babes?"

She licks her lips and blushes. She holds her nose and laughs.

He stares at her with a grin on his face.

"What?" she questions, then lets out another laugh. "Yeah, okay, I do, but it depends on who, but I rather it be given to me."

He says to himself, *'Shit, I'm sure I'm gonna have to lick it before I can stick it.'* He shakes his head and decides, *'Nah, it's not gonna be that type of party.'* But what felt like a sharp bite from *The Dog*, which needs to ejaculate tonight, makes him swallow some spit and say, "So what about if I was to offer to go down on you now? What would you say?"

She does not say yes or nod. She only smiles and slides her body further down on the sofa.

He grabs the waist of her skirt and pulls it and her thongs down. He spreads her legs apart and sticks his face between her thighs.

Chapter 10

MONDAY EVENING AND ESCHEWAL sits at his desk, bored as hell, waiting for the time to hit six. His thoughts travel back to the weekend. He sees himself licking Camille's vagina.

He hates *The Dog* in him. He clenches his teeth and feels like spitting as the smell of her vagina comes to his memory. When the scent first hit him, he wanted to scream, *"Err, it stinks."* but could not bring himself to embarrass her, so he held his breath, closed his eyes, and licked.

After the ordeal, he swore he would never do oral sex again, and what made it worse was that he only did it thinking he had to, not realizing she would have given him sex with or without oral.

He rubs his chin and readjusts himself in the chair. He opens and closes a few programs on his screen to make it seem like he is working and then relaxes as his manager leaves the office for the day.

He sucks his teeth. He knows *The Dog* will take over his life if he does not do something or think of something to control *The Dog*. He shakes his head; he wishes some miracle could happen to make him become a creator of values right now.

He questions himself, *'Why? How?'* His thoughts now travel back to a section in the black book. It is a section on romantic love.

One of life's greatest achievements is finding true romantic love, then committing oneself to a monogamous relationship.

For a moment, his mind goes blank, and then it hits him. He thinks, *'I haven't become a creator of values because I haven't found romantic love and began a monogamous relationship.'*

He is sure this is why. He did everything else the black book instructed, except this. He tells himself, *'Yep, I'm gonna begin my search for romantic love.'*

His faith in the black book restores. *The Dog* retreats to its cage. He feels at ease, and before deciding where to begin his search, Deuce's name flashes up on his phone.

Eschewal flips into his player dialogue and answers, "Yeah, what's going on, bruv?"

"Nothing, man, wha gwan?"

"I'm at work innit, soon finish in about ten minutes. Oi, you listening? What happened with that ting on Friday?"

"Nothing, man. She's an idiot, everything criss, man. She try question me, but she never know nothing."

A smile reaches Eschewal's face. He had been agonizing all weekend over it; he now promises himself he will never do anything like that again.

"Anyway, listen," begins Deuce, "what you doing on the weekend?"

"Nothing. Why?"

"Boy, there's something in the park innit, ber girls are gonna be there, bruv."

Another smile hits Eschewal's face. He feels this could be a perfect place to find romantic love. "Yeah, man, I'm down. Just call me at the weekend, innit."

Chapter 11

THE WEEKEND ARRIVES. THE sun blazes hot as Eschewal backs his car into a tight parking space and switches off the engine.

Deuce pops the door and says, "Come we go."

Eschewal pops his door and steps out. He slams it shut and turns on the alarm, then follows.

As he and Deuce hit the park area, they join a thick crowd of people walking toward the main stage. Loud music pumps. Different food aromas waft through the air. People jump up and down, dancing to the loud music, spilling their drinks on themselves and others.

Eschewal and Deuce stop on the outskirts of the massive crowd of ravers.

Deuce's eyes dart around at all the females. He says to himself, *'Nothing but jezzys.'*

Eschewal's eyes move from girl to girl, studying them like beautiful works of art on display in a gallery. Three minutes more, and he would never have seen her. But at that moment, when he decided to look over his shoulder, his world would never be the same again.

Everything around him falls silent for some seconds, and his eyes become transfixed on love. She stands, glowing and radiating her beauty. A sharp prick sticks him in his heart like an arrow from the love cupid. His stomach tightens as if being pulled together by a leather belt. His legs feel as if he has done a million squats. He seems to have lost control of his bodily functions. His heart seems to tell him; *this is your future wife. You need to be stepping to her now.* But the fear of rejection makes him turn around to contemplate his actions. He can feel his heart pounding. He believes it is too good to be true that he could find romantic love so easily.

He shakes his head. *'I don't deserve someone as nice as her. I can't get someone like her, and she'll probably have a boyfriend anyway.'* He closes his eyes, and a passage from the black book filters through his mind: *One must learn to love oneself and realize that there is no perfect person whom one must live up to. Love can be found anywhere and at any time. When you see it, you must seize the moment.*

The words from the black book dispel his rationalizations and wash away his fear. He turns back around to make his move on his dream. Disappointment pulls the corners of his mouth towards his chin; the girl has vanished. He steps a few paces forward, looking through the crowd to spot where the girl has gone. He cannot see her. He feels as if his heart has sunk to his feet.

He turns back towards Deuce, with the feeling of his brain pulsating in his skull from stress. He wants to get away and look for the girl, but he is embarrassed to come out and say he is no longer a player. Besides, he knows Deuce will only laugh at him and say something negative like, "Come on, bruv, don't run down, no girl. Don't be a dickhead. Be a player, man."

Eschewal's mind works overtime to find an excuse to slip away from Deuce when three guys, who all greet Deuce, interrupt his thinking.

Deuce does not introduce Eschewal, so he says, "Hey, bruv, I'll be back in a minute, yeah."

Deuce nods as Eschewal slips away into the crowd.

Chapter 12

AS ESCHEWAL STOPS BY a bridge that leads outside the park, he beats himself up, *'Why did I take so long to step to her? After all, she was going to be my wife? I had nothing to fear.'*

He closes his eyes, and even though the sun is scorching, he feels as if heavy lead-like freezing rain is pelting down, drowning him in sorrow. He opens his eyes, wishing a miracle would float the girl past him, but all he sees is a swarm of colorfully dressed people scrambling out of the park.

He dwells, *'I wonder what ends she comes from?'* He rubs his chin. *'Does she even come from the ends or even from the country? She must come from the ends.'*

He takes out his phone and calls Deuce as he walks back to his car. He tells Deuce to meet him there.

It is not long before Deuce gets to the car with a big smile. "Hey, blood, I just got one fit ting, you know, bruv. Oh shit, she's hectic, one young ting."

Eschewal cannot hide his lack of interest and says in a blunt tone, "Yeah, true stories, yeah?"

Deuce says, "What's wrong with you, blood? Where did you go anyway?"

"Um," begins Eschewal trying to think what to say, "I went for a piss, innit," then with ease, he rolls out his player dialogue, "Then I saw one, ting."

Deuce says, "What, ting?"

"One, ting, one old, ting, innit."

"You gonna link her?"

Dirty Dog

"Nah, nah, it's long. Come we go, man."

Eschewal clicks open the car doors. He and Deuce jump in. Eschewal starts the engine.

Deuce hits him on the shoulder. "Oi, let's drive around for a bit and see if we can pick up some jezzys."

Eschewal pauses with his response; he remembers: *To give up on searching for love is like giving up on life. One must never stop until one finds their romantic love partner.* He looks over at Deuce; he hates acting like a player, but Deuce is his only friend who goes out raving, and he feels that going to raves is the only chance to see the girl again. His embarrassment will not allow him to tell Deuce about his pursuit. Instead, he will pretend to be a player while he attends raves with Deuce, and the moment he finds the girl, he will end the friendship.

Eschewal nods. He puts the car up into gear as thoughts of finding this girl and becoming a creator of values flood his mind. In fact, he no longer cares about becoming a creator of values because he feels this girl alone will give him the love and happiness he has been longing for all his life.

Part Two
Six Months Later

Chapter 13

IT IS FRIDAY AFTERNOON. Eschewal sits at his desk with stress lines etched across his forehead. He has spent half his wages buying new clothes and attending every rave he could get to, and still no sign of the girl in the park.

He looks up from his screen. Both of his eyes are puffy, as if he had been crying. He had not, but behind his eyes, deep within his subconscious, doubt had begun chipping away at the persistence it takes to keep looking for the girl. A smile stretches across his face as desire consumes him. It is overwhelming; it will not let him stop. He has to find her. He still feels she will be his wife and provide him with the happiness he has longed for all his life.

He closes his eyes. His latest dream of him and her sailing towards the sun as they exchange vows emerges clear in his mind, crisp and indestructible. He opens his eyes and stares ahead.

The voice of one of his colleagues snaps him out of his trance. "I've tried it already. No matter how long you stare at it, it won't go any faster."

Eschewal looks toward his colleague and laughs; now, he wishes the time would tick faster so he could leave the office and get to the circuit of wine bars and clubs to fulfill his dream.

This thought brings Deuce to mind. He wishes he had someone else to attend raves with because it is getting harder and harder to pretend to be a player and explain why he is not approaching and talking to any girls. Also, because Deuce always makes his girls bring a friend for him, this causes Eschewal to constantly find ways of making the friends, not like him. Up to now, he has succeeded in not sleeping with any friends. However, tension is brewing because Deuce is beginning to feel used. Eschewal senses it but has to stick to his plan. He will not sleep with anyone because he wants to be fresh when he finds his princess. He thinks he will be a second-time virgin once he has sex with his princess on their honeymoon night.

He smiles and looks up at the clock. The time reads five past five; fifty-five minutes left. He huffs and decides to call Deuce.

Deuce answers the call.

Eschewal leans back on his chair. "Yes, sir, what's going on? Yeah, but what's going on tonight?"

Chapter 14

ESCHEWAL PULLS HIS CAR around the corner and parks close to the kerb. He beeps the horn twice to let Deuce know he has arrived. Ten minutes later, Deuce steps out of his door and moseys over to Eschewal's car. He pops the door and jumps into the seat.

Eschewal turns down the music.

"Wha gwan, blood?"

"Yeah, wha gwan?"

They hit fists.

Eschewal puts the car into gear and then drives towards some type of launch party up in the city.

Deuce leans back in the chair. He rolls down the window. He looks at Eschewal and says, "Hey, blood, you know how much gyal is gonna be at this ting?"

Eschewal turns left onto the main road and then replies with a smile, "Yeah, true stories, yeah?"

"Course, blood, ber gyal. I'm telling you, bruv…" before Deuce can finish his sentence, he spots two fine young females walking. "Oi, bruv, stop, stop," he points at the two young females. "Look at that over there, blood. Stop the car. Let me spit to them."

Eschewal pulls the car over to the left, then swings it around into a U-turn and drives towards the young females. He stops the car beside them. Deuce jumps out and begins his spiel. He never usually does this but wants to point out that he is doing all the work to get the girls.

He jumps back into the car, laughing. "Yeah, blood,

Dirty Dog

those young tings are on it. They said they're gonna link man on the rebound."

Eschewal nods and spins the car back around. Before he can put the car into second gear, Deuce spots another two girls. He tells Eschewal to stop. Deuce hollers out the window to the prettiest one out of the two, "What's going on, babes?"

The girl pushes up her nose, ignores Deuce, and walks on with a sense of conceit in her steps.

Deuce hollers, "Oi, you little bitch, don't try blow me out. Don't try go on like you're stush. Anyway, jog on, your lip long like liver."

Eschewal laughs.

Deuce smiles and says, "You get me, though, blood, she try go on like she's nice for man. With her cheap shoes, come, man, blow."

Eschewal puts the car into gear, turns up the music then pulls away from the kerb. He shoots past the conceited girls in second gear and onwards to the launch party.

Chapter 15

THE STREET LIGHTS ARE a bit brighter as Eschewal enters the city's uptown. Most of the stores are still open, and the streets are packed with people, making it seem as if it is midday and not nearly midnight.

Eschewal looks at Deuce and decides to start a girl conversation to make him think he is still on his wavelength. "Oi, bruv, do you know one chick name? Hold on… I can't even remember her name." He makes up a name; he still cannot remember the name of the girl that he picked up from the bus stop. "Yeah, yeah, Reanne?"

Deuce shakes his head. "Nah, where's she from?"

"I don't even know; I think she's from the ends, still."

Deuce scratches his chin. "Yeah, what about her anyway?"

"Nah, I must've linked her one time, innit," Eschewal shakes his head. "I swear down, bruv, she was stinking, ponging. Ter, but you know what? I was scared to tell her, rudeboy. I just held my nose and pushed it in."

Deuce laughs. "Wait there. What, was she fit?"

Eschewal shrugs. "Nah, not really."

Deuce shakes his head. "Rah, you're selling. If she weren't fit, that's long. Listen, the only way I would brush a ting that's stinking is if she's fit, and she will be a one pop." He sucks his teeth. "Trust me, when I get them butters that stink, I don't ramp to run them out of my yard." He sucks his teeth again. "I tell them straight 'cause how I see it; I'm doing them a favor. As when they sleep with the next man, they will make sure they wash their pussy until it smells like freshwater pussy."

Eschewal laughs. "What's freshwater pussy, blood?"

Deuce looks surprised. "Don't you know, bruv, that when a girl washes her pussy properly and her pH is balanced, it should smell like freshwater." He huffs and continues, "Trust me, that's why I do the finger test. I always do it. If I take my finger out, and it doesn't smell like freshwater." He sucks his teeth once more. "Like I said, if she's fit, it's a one pop. If she's a butters, I don't stop run them. It's nothing long. Trust me, bruv, certain chicks, all they do is wipe out their armpit and spray on deodorant, then run out on the road and wanna jump in man's bed, and talk bout let's get down and dirty." He shakes his head and wipes the corners of his mouth. "It's not that type of party." He looks towards Eschewal with his face screwed and says, "Anyway, how come it's only now you're telling me about this link?" He points his finger. "But you know what, your bad mind, though. You know you ain't link me with nothing since we've been moving."

Eschewal now regrets that he started the conversation. He uses a lie to slip out of Deuce's valid point. "Just cool, man, I'm gonna link you with something soon, just cool."

With the sound of a threat in his voice, Deuce says, "Yeah, you better link man with something soon, bruv."

Eschewal does not reply as he pushes the car, just in time before the traffic lights turn red.

Chapter 16

ESCHEWAL ARRIVES AT THE venue. He cruises past the long line filled with girls. They come in all shapes and sizes, some dressed in high heels and short skirts, others in low heels and short skirts, but all have goose pimples on their legs.

Deuce talks on his phone. He pulls it away from his mouth and points toward the long line of girls; he whispers, "You see how much girl is here, blood?"

Eschewal nods. He takes the first left and looks for a parking space.

Deuce ends his call and repeats his last sentence.

Eschewal replies, "I see it, blood, I see it, ber gyal."

Deuce hits the dashboard. "Forget bout that, you know the ting I was just talking to, said she wants to get chopped by two man."

In an unconcerned manner, Eschewal replies, "Yeah… is that how she's going on? Better that, boy." hoping that Deuce will sense that he is not interested in another one of his threesomes.

Deuce squeezes his lips together as he tries to convince Eschewal that this time will not be like the last time. He wipes the corner of his mouth and begins, "Nah, I'm telling you, blood. I told her I'm gonna come down tonight with a friend, innit, that's you, innit and deal with her case."

Eschewal finds a parking space and rolls his car into the spot.

He looks at Deuce from the corner of his eye and

says, "That's long, man. Doing a battery is long. Look what happened last time. I swear if that girl ever saw my face, we would be in jail now for rape."

Deuce's right eye twitches. He fires back, "Naaaaah, it's different this time, blood. This girl is down; she wants to slam two man. Didn't you hear me talking to her?" He does not wait for Eschewal's reply. He adds, "Trust me, rudeboy, this ting is a big jezz, ber man's wet her, fit as well, blood. If you ever see how fit she is, you'll go mad."

Eschewal turns off the engine and remains quiet. He looks straight ahead. He is lost for words as he struggles to find an excuse.

Deuce believes he has done enough to influence him. He smirks and says, "So what, you down then, yeah?"

Eschewal opens the door and replies, "Yeah, man, whatever, man, I'm down." He shakes his head, hoping he can end his player pretense soon.

Deuce jumps out of his door and says, "Alright, I'm gonna call her back and tell her we're coming tonight."

They slam the car doors and make their way back towards the venue.

Chapter 17

THE VENUE IS FRESH, modern, and classy. Eschewal and Deuce walk past the long line of girls and head for the V.I.P entrance. Eschewal feels like a celebrity as the bouncer opens the red rope for him and Deuce to enter. Eschewal glances over his shoulder, just before he steps through the open glass doors, at the long line of girls. Excitement bubbles up inside of him. He feels he will surely see that girl from the park because everybody that raves seems to be here tonight.

Deuce gives his name to the pretty woman working the guest list. She ticks him off, plus one. He and Eschewal ascend the marble staircase, which leads to the rave. The moment they enter the dance floor, their eardrums become deafened by music that makes them want to dance. People surround the bar waiting to be served while others mingle in small groups around different sections of the room.

Deuce taps Eschewal and points towards the bar. They step over in its direction, but before they can get there, a tall, fresh-faced, well-groomed male stops Deuce. Everything about this man's appearance seems flashy, from the style of his outfit to his watch and the shoes he wears. He smiles a broad smile showing large straight teeth and welcomes Deuce with a hug. They chat for a moment or two. Deuce then turns to Eschewal. "Oi, you know Spiv, innit?"

"Course, man, from the ends," Eschewal greets Spiv

Von Mozar

with a handshake and says, "Yeah, wha gwan, bruv, you safe?"

Spiv replies with a firm nod, but Eschewal does not notice that Spiv's eyes hold a glint of coldness. This is due to Eschewal being the younger brother of a person who used to bully and rob Spiv back in the day.

With a forced smile, Spiv turns to Deuce, looks back at Eschewal, nods, then says, "Alright, peace," and continues walking wherever he is going.

Chapter 18

AFTER BEING SERVED AT the bar, Eschewal follows Deuce to a corner near the female toilets. Eschewal had not realized why the first time Deuce had led him over to the female toilets when they began raving six months ago, but now it all makes sense.

Eschewal's eyes widen as a stream of girls from outside comes in and make their way over to the toilets. His heart beats a little faster. He can feel his stomach muscles contracting as two stunning girls walk his way. His heart slows down. He had thought that one of them was the girl in the park.

As the girls enter the toilets, another wannabe player tries to pull one of them, but she pulls off his grip and enters the toilets with attitude.

Deuce grins. He knows that wannabe player made a fateful mistake. He feels like giving him this advice,*"You need to fall back, player. Never try to pull a female before she can check on herself. You need to relax and wait patiently until she exits, then make your move, gee."* Before the two stunners leave the toilets, two other groups of girls enter, all looking so fresh and so clean Deuce's penis rises. He tries to calm himself, but it is no good. He is like a child in a sweetie shop.

The two stunners exit the toilets and walk back towards Eschewal and Deuce with eyes fixed straight ahead. Before the one in front can get to walk past, Deuce grabs down on her arm. She stops and smiles. He pulls her towards him and begins his spiel.

Dirty Dog

Eschewal looks at the friend. She is almost as pretty as the girl in the park but does not have that special thing. He looks over at Deuce. He knows Deuce needs his help because, at any moment, he feels the friend will feel left out and end up pulling the girl away from Deuce. He takes a deep breath and steps toward the girl. "Hi, what's your name?" he says disinterestedly.

The girl answers with a tone of voice that suggests, *don't do me any favors.*

Eschewal replies, "Sorry, what did you say your name was?"

She rolls the lie off her tongue again, "Leasha."

"Leasha, yeah? That's a beautiful name," he goes for a handshake and introduces himself.

The girl smiles and gives him eye contact.

He senses the girl might be contemplating giving him a chance. He cannot risk that, so he dives in and says, "Can I get your number?"

The girl looks away from him as she replies, "I don't give out my number."

He bites down on his lip. He pretends to lose his voice for a second; he has read the girl correctly. She is the type of girl who has to be talked to with manners, and if you're asking for her number, you have to do it with much more decorum. He plies on the acting. He wrinkles his forehead and says, "Why?"

With another lie, the girl looks at Eschewal and says, "Because I've got a boyfriend, innit."

He smiles and fires back with a mind game question, "How many boyfriends you got, then?" he says with an unconcerned smile.

The girl replies, with a hint of puzzlement in her voice, "Only one…"

He raises his eyebrows. "Is that all?" Then says, "Is there no room for one more?"

The girl flicks her neck. "Nah, sorry, I'm happy," and as Deuce finishes putting her friend's number in his phone, she grabs her friend's arm and disappears into the crowd.

Deuce turns to Eschewal and says, "What, did you get her number?"

Eschewal shakes his head and says, "Nah, she was going on stush," then smiles slightly, happy he avoided another possible distraction. He closes his eyes for a moment and thinks, how many more girls do I have to blow out before I see the girl in the park again? He shoots his eyes back open as Deuce pokes him in the arm.

Deuce is about to give Eschewal another one of his pep talks on playing the game. He wipes the corner of his mouth. "Listen, bruv," he begins, "for man like you, yeah, you need to tell them, pretty girls, a bling, you get me? You have to become Mister Bling with them. You get me?" He takes a sip of his drink and continues, "Tell them something like you're a promoter and wanna add them to your guest list. Then ring them and give them some other chat, take them out for lunch and talk more shit on a business level, and before you know it, you're in their knickers."

Eschewal rolls his eyes and nods as Deuce continues his pep talk.

Chapter 19

ESCHEWAL AND DEUCE ARE now outside in the cold fresh air, which hits Eschewal from all directions. It feels good on his skin. His nostrils expand as he sucks in deep breaths of fresh air, giving his lungs the oxygen they need after inhaling second-hand smoke for over three hours.

A pretty girl with a tiny head, short hair, tall and slim walks past the guys. Deuce hits Eschewal on the shoulder and laughs. "Oi, you see that girl, yeah?" He does not wait for Eschewal to reply. "Listen, cuz, she's some materialistic bitch. Try not link me back when I told her I wasn't driving. All try not even answer my call, bruv." His mouth corners turn into a frown at the thought of the girl seeing his number and just letting it ring. He continues, "Yeah, blood, she try take man for fool, until she saw me in my new ride. Then she start ringing off my phone. Yeah, I linked her, then sexed her in my car, and that was it, never linked her back again or answered her calls." He laughs. "Yeah, little bitch."

Eschewal throws his keys in the air and catches them. "Seen, I hear that, bruv. Certain girls love to play too much games."

The guys cross over the road where Eschewal parked his car.

Deuce says, "I'm glad you know that, blood, and you due to know that you can't make them drag you into their sick game. You have to have a tight lid on your emotions, blood. Because you know how many times I wanted to text her a nasty message? If I ever did that, bruv," He shakes his head, "I would have never got too wet, her. You get me?"

Eschewal nods and says, "True stories."

They fall quiet.

As they reach the car, Deuce receives a text. It is from a girl he has been dating for the past six months but has not managed to have sex with yet. He hopes that she may be ready to have sex with him now. So he forgets about the girl who wants a threesome and decides he cannot pass up this opportunity. He puts his phone in his pocket and jumps in the car with Eschewal.

Chapter 20

AS ESCHEWAL STICKS THE clutch; Deuce sends a message back to the girl; he tells her to call him. Within thirty seconds, she calls back.

He answers, "Yeah, what's up, babes...? Yeah, I'm still coming...? Where do you live again? Alright, darling, I'll be there in about half an hour." He huffs. He now must pretend this girl is the girl who wants the threesome, which is a risk because she might not give him any sex when she sees he has brought a friend. However, He believes his silver tongue is capable of talking her around. His eyes look worried. He wonders if Eschewal will think the girl's house is too far to travel to at this time of the night. He tells him.

Eschewal replies, "Blood, I never know she lives way over there. That's far, bruv." He shakes his head, happy that he now has an excellent angle to escape another distraction from his goal. "Cuz, trust me, that's long. I'm not even feeling that, bro. And then man has to drive back afterwards."

Tension runs through Deuce; you can hear it in his voice, "Ah, come on, bruv, don't sell it, man's gonna fuck pussy, you know."

Those words awaken *The Dog* in Eschewal. He has not had sex for such a long time. He has been controlling the urges of *The Dog* with thoughts of the girl in the park. The memory of the girl floods his mind. He visualizes her straight white teeth, beautiful slender hands, and feet.

Deuce feels that Eschewal is fighting his mental demons and dives in with his hard sell, "Come on, man, if you ever see how fit this girl is, you know it's gonna be worth it, blood. Trust me. I'm not even lying, she's got some big tits with a massive cock-bottom, and on top of that, she's det, blood. Content, she's a sort."

Eschewal shakes his head, pumps the brakes, and stops in front of an all-night off-licence. "Boy, I don't know, bruv. I don't even feel for it." He pauses, then uses his best excuse, "Because, look what happened last time, you think I wanna go jail for rape? It's long."

"What did I tell you, blood? It's not like that this time. The girl is down, trust me." Deuce dips into his pocket, takes out his phone, and flicks to the message from the girl who wants the threesome. "Look, blood," he shows Eschewal the message, which reads: IF UR FRIEND LOOKS AS GOOD AS U THEN WE CAN FUK. "Listen, bruv," begins Deuce, in a more confident voice, "I'll even drive back," as he ends that sentence, his phone rings. It is the girl who wants the threesome, but he pretends it is the pretty girl with the small head. "You see; it's that idiot ting we just saw." He ends the call. A few seconds later, his phone rings again. "Ah, suck yourself," he yells to the phone and lets it ring out. He turns to Eschewal and says, "So what you saying, blood, you down?"

Eschewal nods in defeat.

Deuce jumps out of the car. He runs into the off-licence to buy condoms and alcohol. He runs back to the car. He gets in and leads Eschewal into another night of escaping a sexual situation.

Chapter 21

THE WALK TOWARDS THE girl's front door has Eschewal feeling like he is floating as if he is experiencing some out-of-body sensation. He thinks of ways to sour the surroundings once inside the house. *'Maybe I will not talk or answer any questions.'* Before he can decide what to do, the girl answers the door.

Straight away, he knows she is not expecting to see someone with Deuce. Her eyes look toward him with a hint of coldness. She cannot believe Deuce has taken this liberty and brought another man to her home. A chill comes over her; she thinks Deuce must have found out about her past. Anger storms through her while images of her having a threesome flash in her mind. She feels like spitting as she remembers sticking her tongue in a guy's anus. The taste of feces fills her memory, and the hate she felt for herself at that moment while giving that guy analingus pours out of her as she looks into the sex-mad eyes of Deuce.

She feels like crying. She had hoped that Deuce might be interested in having a serious relationship with her. *"Bastard,"* she says to herself. *"If it's a battery you want, that's what you're gonna get, along with a rape charge."*

She releases a smile onto her sensuous lips. She curls her right hand into a fist behind her back and says, "Aren't you coming in?"

Dirty Dog

Deuce steps up a step and says, "Yeah, of course. I was waiting for you to invite me in."

She looks at Eschewal and says to Deuce, "Who's your friend?"

Deuce turns to Eschewal and then looks back at her. "Oh, that's my brethren, Eros. Oi, come, blood," he orders.

Eschewal nods towards the girl, walks up the six steps behind Deuce, and then enters the house.

The girl loosens the fist and shuts the door. She directs Deuce and Eschewal toward the living room. She's planning to make them pay for all the sins she has been subjected to by the men in her life.

Chapter 22

THE LIVING ROOM IS neat and smells sweet. Deuce and Eschewal sit down on the blue leather sofa. The girl has not yet entered the living room. She is outside the door listening to Eschewal and Deuce's plan.

Deuce says in a high whisper, "Listen, blood, this is what we're gonna do. Give her some drink and put it on her, because at the end of the day, even though she wants to do it, she might still be a bit boomee. You get me? We got to convince her."

Eschewal looks at Deuce with vexation on his face. "Hold on, bruv. I thought you said she was down? We don't have to convince her of nothing if she's down."

Deuce sits back on the couch and replies philosophically, "Check it, yeah, if someone walks into a sweetie shop and comes across ber new sweets they've never tasted before, it's up to the shopkeeper to convince that person that the sweets taste good and are worth buying. If the shopkeeper fails to convince that person, the person will just walk out of the shop without buying anything. You get me? We are the shopkeepers, and it's up to us to convince her to give us her pussy."

Eschewal scratches his head, shakes it from side to side, sucks his teeth, and sits back on the sofa. "Yeah, whatever, blood, whatever."

The living room door opens. The girl walks in, swaying her hips and balancing a tray with three glasses.

Von Mozan

Under the brightness of the light bulb, her full beauty shines. Eschewal did not realize how beautiful she really was; the girl is stunning, and on top of that, her body could beat most bodies belonging to famous superstars. Cold chills run down his spine as he sees what seems like a cunning plan in her eyes. He cannot place it, so he shrugs it off.

The girl puts the tray on the coffee table and sits on the blue leather armchair opposite Eschewal and Deuce. She says as she licks her lips, "Do you lot bun greens?"

Deuce and Eschewal shake their heads.

Deuce says, "Nah, but we got drink, innit." He reaches for the bottle of brandy and, with a steady hand, pours it into the glasses.

The girl watches as Deuce pours. She also wanted them to be smokers, for it would look even better to a judge and jury that they also came with drugs. *'Not to worry,'* she thinks, *'the alcohol should be enough to convict a pair of low-lives.'*

Within the next half hour, the girl has drunk more than half of the bottle. She seems drunk but at the same time in control of what she is saying and doing.

Eschewal has not touched his glass and sits there listening to Deuce talking nonsense.

Deuce stands up and says, "Come, babes. Let me talk to you outside."

The girl giggles and says, "I hope you've got something good to say to me?"

Deuce pulls her up and leads her outside.

Chapter 23

ESCHEWAL IS LEFT IN the living room, contemplating how to dodge another sexual situation.

Deuce has the girl in the bathroom, but things are not going his way. The girl has sobered up enough to execute her plan of making Deuce force himself on her.

He says, "Why you going on like you don't want sex?"

She says, "I do want sex."

He smiles. "So let me hit it then, innit."

She grins. "Noooo," she says while pushing him away.

He sucks his teeth. "Stop going on, silly, man," he says while stepping back to her. He grips her waist and bites down on her neck. She moans. He whispers in her ear, "I know what you want. You want a threesome, innit?"

She smiles, then pauses in her thoughts and remembers her wild days. It makes her sick to think of them, but it seems that they would always haunt her. *'Why can't people believe that people can change their spots?'* she wonders. All she wants in life now is to have a serious relationship. She feels like crying; her inner emotions feel torn. She swallows and answers, "Yeah, maybe."

Deuce's eyes show surprise. He expected her to say no; then, he would have asked her, *"Would you like to try?"* Instead, he says, "Do you want me to call

Dirty Dog

brethren?"

With a cheeky giggle, she replies, "Yeah, if you want."

He puts his hand underneath her skirt. "Okay, in a minute, let me take a quick feel first."

She laughs and pulls his hand out. "Aren't you gonna call your brethren?"

He licks his lips. "Yeah, but let me hit it first, man."

The Dog in Deuce seems to growl, and in a hurry, he pulls his penis out, but before he can roll on a condom, his semen spits out all over him.

"Shit, aren't you gonna put it in?" she asks as she licks her lips and rubs her clitoris.

He clears his throat. "I have to get a condom. Hold on. I'm gonna call my brethren as well." He exits the bathroom and bursts into the living room, sweating.

Eschewal looks up. "What, did you hit it?"

He replies, "Course, bro, she got that tight-gripper. Listen, she's in the bathroom waiting for you."

Eschewal hesitates before he gets up.

Deuce says, "What, get up then, don't you want any pussy?"

Eschewal does not reply. He exits the room leaving Deuce to clean himself off.

Chapter 24

ESCHEWAL CALMS HIS HEART rate as he steps into the bathroom. His body cries out for sex. The sight of the girl sitting on the sink with her legs spread meets his eyes. He blinks, and as a sensation that feels like *The Dog* is howling for the desired flesh, he mumbles, "Shit," and steps further into the bathroom.

In a quiet tone, the girl says, "So, it's your turn to take me now, yeah?"

Eschewal freezes and replies, sounding out every syllable. "Not if you don't want me to. You don't, do you?"

She shakes her head and whispers something that sounds like, "No."

The weight of *The Dog's* need falls off Eschewal's shoulders. "Alright," he begins as he nods, "I understand. You don't even know me. Listen, I'm gonna call Deuce to come back in, yeah?"

Not looking back, he flees the bathroom with much relief, leaving the girl looking puzzled and fuming that she is now unable to call rape.

Eschewal walks back into the living room.

Deuce sniggers and then says, "Ain't she gonna make you go thru?"

Eschewal lies. "Yeah, but I'm just gonna get a condom in the car."

Deuce smiles, then fronts, "Alright. Oi, get me one as well, yeah."

Von Mozan

Eschewal nods. "Yeah, alright, bro. I'll be back in a second." He hits the pavement and strides over to his car. He gets in, starts the engine, and drives off, leaving Deuce on the other side of the city.

Chapter 25

HALF AN HOUR LATER Eschewal is back in his town. He feels relieved that he controlled *The Dog* back in the girl's bathroom. If she did not say, in a sinister way, "So, it's your turn to take me now, yeah?" he would have sex with her.

He looks into his rearview mirror; his reflection shows a man who looks like he is about to be beaten by *The Dog*. He shakes his head and thinks, *'this task, this goal, it's too big for me.'* He feels that in the following situation he encounters, *The Dog* may win. As the feeling leaves him and he turns off the main road taking a sharp left, coming towards him is the corruption of the rotten core of the city. His eyes meet with the corruption. He visualizes *The Dog* ripping out of his body, its face twisting in a grotesque form, growling and foaming at the mouth.

He grits his teeth and continues driving. His eyes dart into the rearview mirror.

The corruption waves at him.

He directs his eyes back to the road and tries to fight this filthy temptation. His eyes dart back to the rearview mirror, his foot pumps the brake, and the car halts at the top of the road.

It is too much; *The Dog* has won tonight. With his heart pounding, he reverses the car to satisfy *The Dog*.

The temptation of corruption runs up toward his car. He feels his stomach twist. He hates himself already for the deed he is about to do, but *The Dog* demands that he comply. He has no control.

He glances into his rearview mirror.

The corruption has stopped running and is walking over to another car.

He closes his eyes and says, "Thank you." He opens his eyes and watches as the corruption gets into the car, leaving him alone to face his demons.

He takes a deep breath and pulls back into the road. He shakes his head, knowing he needs to find the girl in the park before he lets himself slip into the world's corruption.

Chapter 26

ESCHEWAL SITS AT HIS desk. Thoughts of the nasty action he would have done at the weekend explode in his mind. He wants to slam his fist on the desk and scream, *"WHY!"* but he knows why he lost control, so he relaxes and meditates.

The key to controlling destructive behavior is to fill one's life with productive forms of stimulation that outweigh the destructive behavior's stimulation.

Eschewal slides his finger down his nose and huffs. He knows he will be in big trouble if he does not find the girl in the park. He believes she is his only hope to provide a productive source of stimulation greater than *The Dog's* urge for promiscuous sex.

A colleague of his flips him out of his meditation. "Are you alright, mate?"

Eschewal looks up to the voice and dons a false smile. "Yeah, I'm alright. I've just got a few things on my mind."

"Is it anything I can help you with?" enquires the colleague.

"Nah, I'm sweet, mate," replies Eschewal with a wink.

The colleague smiles. "Oh, I see, women trouble, ah?"

Eschewal nods. "Yeah, something like that."

The colleague nods and then continues with whatever he is doing, leaving Eschewal to his thoughts.

Von Mozan

As if creeping from the bottom of his heart, sadness spreads across Eschewal's face. The dream of waking up in the morning with the girl in the park as his wife and dressing their children for school is dissolving each day.

He squeezes his eyes together as he fights back tears. He lowers his head and wipes his eyes. He repeats to himself, *"Be strong, be strong, don't give up. Life has to give you what you demand. You will find her."*

His phone vibrates. He looks at the caller ID. Deuce is calling him again to awaken *The Dog*. He bites down on his lip and pushes down the anger rising inside him. The phone stops vibrating. He receives a message. He listens to it. Deuce offers him free entry to an exclusive club that only admits the rich and famous, along with a few other lucky souls.

He does not want to go. He needs to take a break from Deuce because tempting *The Dog* in him with all those sexual encounters is not helping his goal.

He rubs his head. He knows he will be going because he would not forgive himself if he did not go and the girl in the park had been there.

Chapter 27

THE NIGHT STREETS ARE fresh from a recent downpour. Eschewal is a road away from Deuce's home. He hates raving on a weeknight, but this is the sacrifice he has to make to fulfill his dream. He stops, parks, and waits outside Deuce's house.

As usual, Deuce makes him wait a while. Finally, he exits his house and then jumps in the car. He brings along a smile and a laugh. He says, "What's up, me brudder? Everything cool, yeah?"

Eschewal looks towards him and says, "Course man, you done know," and covers his hand over Deuce's clenched fist. Eschewal pauses for a second waiting to see if Deuce will mention what happened at the weekend.

Deuce does not and is trying his best not to, so as Eschewal moves through the city towards the nightclub, he bites his tongue from saying, *"Oi, bruv, you're a waste-man, you know? How can you leave man on the other side of town? Do you know what I had to do to get home? Not to mention the lies I had to feed my girl."* He sucks his teeth and looks through the car window at all the alluring storefronts whizzing past.

Deuce still needs Eschewal to drive him around. He will only get rid of him once his girlfriend or her people become aware of Eschewal's car.

In the meantime, he will plot how to get Eschewal back for deserting him.

He looks over at Eschewal and then back on the

road as Eschewal turns left along the road leading to the club.

Chapter 28

AFTER PARKING THE CAR two streets away, Eschewal and Deuce do a slow walk back to the venue. There is no rush because they would have to wait in the queue regardless of whether their names were on the guest list or not.

No more than ten minutes later, they find themselves inside. The first thing Eschewal notices about this club is the color of the walls and the furniture. They affect the eye and tell the brain to relax and get comfortable. This is precisely what he does; his state of well-being goes into the happiness mode.

Deuce taps him on the shoulder and tells him he will be back in a moment. Eschewal gives him a smile and a nod. Deuce disappears into the back of the club.

Eschewal steps off towards the bar, and from a distance, he thinks it is her, the girl in the park. His body feels weak, his palms sweat, and hairs on the back of his neck stand up. He reaches the bar and realizes it is not the girl in the park. A feeling of lust enters him, and he contemplates talking to the girl because she has the qualities: the beautiful hands, feet, and straight teeth. He pauses and takes a second to study how she is dressed. He locks his gaze on her see-through black shirt, which stops just above her belly button. The top four buttons are undone, exposing her cleavage. He rests his elbow on the bar and watches her dance.

Von Mozan

She wines up and down with long slender arms above her head. This movement makes her supple breasts move with a life of their own.

His eyes make contact with her jeans; her sexy, succulent, slim legs fill them out, designed to turn on any red-blooded man.

His eyes drop to her open-toe high-heeled shoes, revealing her toes free from corns and calluses.

He nods, and at that moment, he sees the girl as nothing more than another addictive, destructive drug. The urge to talk to her disappears. It is replaced with a total focus on finding his princess.

He turns towards the bar and orders a glass of orange juice.

Chapter 29

IN THE V.I.P BAR, Deuce and Spiv are in conversation. Deuce says, "Oi, bruv, this is big, you know. How did you get this link?"

"Didn't I tell you, when I was in pen, I saved my cellmate from getting robbed, innit."

Deuce shakes his head.

Spiv continues, "Yeah, two dick heads from West rolled up in the cell gassed, gassing and try to peel his kettle, innit. I just wile them up and run them out the cell." Spiv sips his drink, then continues, "Yeah, it turned out my cellmate was a millionaire, and the watch those pricks tried to suck was given to him by his dad on his deathbed."

Deuce's eyes widen.

Spiv continues, "Yeah, true stories, the man was all crying after and thanking me, then promises he will drop some pees on me when I get out, innit."

Deuce smiles. "Oh, seen. So is this the same man you told me about who owns all these clubs?"

Spiv nods. "Yeah, bruv. He owns this one, innit. He owns hotels and ber clubs. He's even given me a club to manage. So I'll be starting a new weekly club night in a hot minute."

Deuce flicks his head upwards. "Seen, is that how you're going on? Yes, big dog." The guys hits fist.

Spiv gulps his drink and says with cold eyes, "Oi, you know you should stop moving with that teefing yute."

Dirty Dog

Deuce's eyes show surprise. "Which teefing, yute?"

Spiv points his finger. "Eros, innit. You shouldn't move with them, boy, there. I don't trust him and none of his family. They're all teefs."

The coldness in Spiv's eyes returns as memories of being bullied and robbed by Eschewal's older brother comes to him. But what burned him was getting his girls stolen by Eschewal's older brother. The breaking point came for him when Eschewal's older brother had sex with one of his girls and stretched out her vagina. When he slept with her afterward, he felt the difference, she felt it too, and that was the last time he ever felt her. Since then, he has had a big insecurity about his penis size. He feels it has not grown since he was a little boy, and no matter how old he gets, he still feels like a little boy. He never makes a girl touch him until he has an erection and the lights are off. Then immediately after sex, he swiftly exits the bedroom to put on extra loose boxer shorts to hide his shriveled penis. He bites down on his lip.

Deuce stands up straight and sucks his teeth. "Yeah, I know he's a cunt, I know he's not safe, but I'm just using him as my lift-boy, innit. Because you dun know, man has to be one step ahead of wifey, can't make her spot any chicks in my car, you get me?"

Spiv laughs and returns to Eschewal, "Oi, you remember how him and his family used to live in that dutty mash-down yard? Their yard used to stink, you know."

Deuce cracks up laughing. "Yeah, I know, I know, grimy."

Spiv smiles. "Come, man, let's go back down to the club."

As they exit the room, Deuce says to Spiv, "What, blood have you got thru on that chick yet, Manna?"

"Nah, bro. I'm still working on it, but as soon as I

Von Mozar

get it, I'm gonna wok it then diss it for making me wait so long. You know how we do, player."

They laugh in unison and walk down the stairs.

Chapter 30

SPIV AND DEUCE ENTER the dance floor. Deuce spots Eschewal by the bar. He taps Spiv and points out Eschewal. The two make their way over to the bar.

Deuce greets Eschewal with, "What's up, bro? What you smiling for?"

The grin disappears from Eschewal's face for a few seconds and then returns. He replies, "It's nothing, man, just cool, man. What's going on?"

Deuce shrugs.

Spiv comes into Eschewal's view; he dons a fake smile. As much as it hurts him, he must convince Eschewal that he likes him. He goes into acting mode. "What you saying, blood?" Spiv rubs his fist on Eschewal's fist, then looks at Deuce. "Oi, you know that I know him from long time, innit?"

Deuce nods.

Spiv continues, looking back at Eschewal, "Yeah, man, you're my brethren. Come, let me buy you a drink. What, you drinking?" Spiv turns to Deuce. "What you drinking, cuz?"

"Anything, man," replies Deuce.

Spiv leans on the bar. The attendant walks up to him straight away, ignoring the other customers. Spiv gives his first two orders, then turns to Eschewal. "What do you want, blood?"

Eschewal shakes his head. "Boy, bruv, I don't even really drink, cuz."

Dirty Dog

Spiv retorts, "How you mean, man? Drink something, man. You can't come to the bar and order a soft drink. Long, you feel me?"

Eschewal scratches his head; he feels a bit intimidated by the peer pressure but remains calm. He flicks his nose and says, "Boy, that's me, bruv, you gotta respect that."

Spiv laughs, not a disrespectful laugh but a friendlier one, then says, *"Just cool, man, show love and drink with the man-dem."* He smiles. "Alright, listen, I bought some champs. I'm gonna get a box juice, just mix that with the champs, then bubble, yeah?"

Eschewal cannot be bothered to argue, so Spiv gets in the drinks.

Spiv whispers into Eschewal's ear. He says he can get any girl in the club he wants. This is not far from the truth; to prove it, he points out three attractive females at the opposite end of the bar. He singles out the most attractive one and says to Eschewal, "You know that's content, innit? If you want that, man can link you with that, you know."

Eschewal wants to press down on his earlobes and block out *The Dog's* barking. He bites his lip. The female Spiv is talking about is stunningly beautiful, but the thought of him fulfilling his dream controls *The Dog*.

The three attractive females come over. Eschewal hopes they will not be interested in what Spiv is saying to them.

Ten minutes later, Eschewal finds himself driving to a penthouse with the three attractive females following in tow.

Chapter 31

INSIDE ESCHEWAL'S CAR IS quiet until Deuce breaks the silence. He says, "Oi, you lot, who's got condoms?"

No one answers.

Deuce repeats himself, "Oi, ain't you lot got no condoms?"

Eschewal shakes his head.

Spiv says, "Just chill, man. We deal with that when we get there, man."

Deuce turns towards the back seat and says to Spiv, "How you mean we deal with that when we get there? We need some boots now, blood. It come in like you wanna play with death?"

"Nah, what I'm saying is that room service can bring that."

Deuce turns back in his seat. "Alright, that's what I wanna hear because there're chicks out on road walking around with disease up their skirt. Trust me. You ever slip with one of these hoes you slide all the way to your grave, you feel me?"

No one replies to Deuce's words of wisdom. He then turns the conversation, "Oi, who's taking which one?"

No one says anything.

He says, "Boy, I want the one wearing the short skirt, blood." He is talking about the most attractive female; he always has to have the best.

Spiv grits his teeth as he knows Deuce will do

anything within his power until he gets the most attractive one. He tries to put Deuce off because he wants to pair the most attractive female with Eschewal. "That ting is on Eros's case, blood, it come in like you didn't see?"

Deuce laughs. "Listen, I never see nothing, blood. It's every man for himself. Man's free to make his move, blood; it's nothing." He looks over at Eschewal. "Oi, bruv, do you want that ting then, yeah?"

Eschewal stops the car at a pair of traffic lights. "Boy, whatever, whoever, blood. I'm not bothered," he lies. His thoughts break as the lights change. He lifts the clutch and moves off.

Spiv says, "Take the next left up there. The hotel is at the end of the road."

Eschewal turns left. He looks in his rearview mirror to check if the three attractive females are still behind him. They are, so he continues driving down the long road.

Chapter 32

THE THREE ATTRACTIVE FEMALES follow up closely behind. The driver is named Soshana. The one sitting in the passenger seat is called Yashima, and the most attractive one, with the short skirt, is named Tanisha. They are all first cousins.

They haven't stopped talking since they left the club. The conversation is now on whom out of Eschewal, Deuce, or Spiv has the biggest penis.

Yashima goes first. She laughs as she says, "Nah, nah, I think, yeah. Spiv's got the biggest dick; you know why? I had a boyfriend the same height as him, and I swear his dick almost reached down to his knee."

Soshana retorts, "Yeah, so what? I fucked a guy who was shorter than the other one. What's his name, Deuce, and his dick went past his knee."

Yashima snaps, "That doesn't mean his dick was bigger. It could have been the same size or even a bit shorter and just looked longer because it has a shorter way to travel down his leg."

Soshana waves her hand in Yashima's face and says, "You're chatting shit, man, innit, T, ain't she chatting S?"

Tanisha is brought into the debate. She replies, looking very comfortable in the back seat. "Listen, what I would say is this: I've fucked lots and lots of guys, and no matter their height, build, or looks, their dicks come in all sizes. Like, I've had real short,

Dirty Dog

skinny guys, but when they take out their cocks, it's as long and thick as my arm. And then I've had tall, muscular men with short, skinny dicks and vice versa. So what it's really about is this: some men are blessed with well-built dicks no matter what their body looks like, and some men are not. Don't forget you know the dick has muscle inside it, and you see how some bres never have to go to the gym to build up their muscles and get them big. The same thing goes for bres with big dicks."

Soshana and Yashima burst out laughing.

Yashima says, "What you saying then, girl, men with small dicks can get them big by doing exercise?"

Tanisha wipes the smile off her face and says, "Well, it stands to reason, innit? If a guy can get the muscles in his arms to grow big by doing exercise. He must also can get the muscles in his dick to grow big." Tanisha looks out of the window and smiles to herself. "Anyway, I've heard it's been done and that there is some special dick work-out program that men can do. For real, if you've got a small dick, do something about it."

All the girls laugh in unison.

Soshana pulls the car over to the kerb in front of the hotel.

Yashima says, "Alright, you lot, who's choosing who because I'm saying, Spiv."

Soshana chooses Deuce and Tanisha chooses Eschewal. Then Yashima says, "Remember how it works. You have to swallow the dick and see how much hand space you have left at the bottom and whoever has the most wins."

Soshana says, "Oi, I hope these guys' dicks ain't cheesy, you know? Because I'm sick and tired of them bres who wanna ask for head and their dicks are cheesy." Soshana curls her top lip. "I'm sure some

Von Mozar

guys with foreskin don't know they need to pull it back and wash underneath it. Err, long."

Yashima replies, "Nah, my girl, if they've got it, they pull it back. They're sweet boys, my girl."

Soshana takes the key out of the ignition. "They better be and remember, yeah, whoever loses buys the rounds."

The girls agree and jump out of the car, laughing.

Chapter 33

SPIV AND DEUCE WERE already out of the car when the girls stopped and got out of theirs. They have not noticed that Eschewal has not yet gotten out of his car. He looks into his rearview mirror and sees them joking and laughing. Deuce is already whispering in Tanisha's ear; Spiv tries to distract Tanisha from Deuce but fails.

Eschewal's eyes follow them as they all walk up the stairs towards the hotel doors. It seems they don't realize that he is not with them. He thinks if they all walk through the hotel doors without still realizing, he will count to thirty and then go.

Everyone except Deuce enters the hotel. He stops atop the stairs and looks down towards the car. He shrugs and says, "What's going on, fam?"

Eschewal does not reply. He pulls the key out of the ignition and pops the door open.

Deuce walks back down the stairs towards the car.

As Eschewal gets out and shuts the door, Deuce repeats himself, "What's going on, fam? Aren't you coming up?"

Eschewal pauses before replying. He wants to say, *"Bruv, I'm not feeling the vibe, I wanna go home,"* but knows Deuce will make him feel guilty by saying, *"Bruv, that's bad mind, why you cock blocking for?"*

So instead, he says, "Yeah, man, I just finished talking to someone on the phone, innit. Then I tried to see if I had any condoms in the car, but I haven't got any."

Deuce flicks his fingers towards the floor and says, "Just cool, man. Spiv said we can get some from room service." He turns his head towards the hotel and then back to Eschewal. "Come, man," he orders with a laugh, "you going on like you don't want no pussy."

Spiv appears at the hotel door. You can hear the fear in his voice as he says, "Shit, I thought you lot had gone, boy."

Deuce replies, "Nah, man. Everything is cool, fam. Come, let's beat up some pussy."

He leads the way over to the check-in desk and wraps his arm around Tanisha's waist. She does not resist and rubs her butt cheek against his crotch.

Soshana and Yashima look at each other and whisper, "She's such a little tart. Why can't she play a little hard to get?"

Spiv, without anyone noticing, glares at Deuce and then focuses on the concierge. He confirms his reserved penthouse suite, which is kept for him two days during the week and one day at the weekend.

The concierge hands over the key to Spiv as vexation falls from Spiv's face. He feels he will not be able to pair Tanisha with Eschewal as planned. This makes him not want to go up to the penthouse. He shakes his head, turns around, then bellows, "You lot ready, yeah? Okay, let's go and have some fun."

Chapter 34

$\mathcal{E}$VERYBODY BUNDLES INTO THE penthouse. Eschewal steps in last. He closes the door and pads towards the lounge. Nerves shoot through him as he feels there will be no way to escape this sexual situation unless he lets everyone know he has been searching for a girl he saw in the park and does not want to have sex with anyone else except her. He can hear them laughing and turning his romantic pursuit into something ugly, like stalking. He swallows his nerves and decides that if there is no way out and he ends up having sex with one of the girls, he will end his search for the girl in the park.

He gets a surprise in the lounge; the girls are no longer flirting but huddled together on a small sofa.

He looks over at Deuce and Spiv, sitting on a long curved sofa opposite the girls. He mouths, "What, everything flop?" For a moment, a smile comes to his face. It disappears when he realizes what's happening. The girls are not giving up anything until some money is spent.

Spiv knows the drill and gets up from the sofa. "Come, man, let's get this shit started. Do you lot want champs, yeah?"

Tanisha jumps up. "Yeah, that's more like it. I was beginning to think you guys weren't gentlemen," she says with a grin as she follows Spiv over to the phone and rubs his back while he rings room service.

Eschewal looks over at Deuce's vexed face. Deuce

thinks Spiv is trying to sabotage his chance with Tanisha, so he tries to embarrass Spiv.

Deuce leans back into the sofa and yells to Spiv, "Oi, blood, don't bother ordering the cheap shit, you know, man's a baller, blood, you get me?"

Spiv ignores Deuce and orders two bottles of the second most expensive champagne on the list and some oysters. He hangs up the phone. "How you mean don't order no cheap shit? Listen, you and Eros better dip into your pockets because this ain't no freeness," neither Eschewal nor Deuce comments.

Spiv sucks his teeth and scans his eyes over everyone. "Oi, we might as well all get into the Jacuzzi until the champs come." He does not wait for anybody's reply. He holds Tanisha by the waist and walks to the Jacuzzi. As he whispers in Tanisha's ear, Deuce's eyes are burning a jealous hole into his back.

Chapter 35

THE CHAMPAGNE AND OYSTERS arrive; the group is half naked, relaxing in the Jacuzzi. Before getting in, Spiv booms to Eschewal and Deuce, "Oi, make sure you lot leave on your boxers, you know, because I'm not in no batty man ting." He has gone on the offensive because his penis is not ready for company. For some reason, it has shriveled even smaller than usual.

The atmosphere has changed since the girls drank a few drinks. Spiv has his arm around Tanisha and is talking into her ear. Deuce is still burning with jealousy even though he is touching Soshana's round, perfectly formed breasts, maybe too perfect to be real. Yashima is trying her best to get close to Eschewal, but it is not quite working.

Spiv looks over at Eschewal from the corner of his eye. He feels it is time to put his plan into action. He had previously heard that Tanisha was carrying an STD and hoped she would give it to Eschewal. He pushes himself out of the tub, feeling a little more confident that the circulation of warm water has helped to expand his penis. He moves over to Yashima and grabs her hand. "Oi, come here. Let me have a word with you in the bedroom."

Yashima does not resist, and everyone except Tanisha looks surprised. Tanisha paddles over to Eschewal, making Deuce look on in amazement.

Deuce shakes his head and whispers in Soshana's

ear, and seconds later, both get out of the Jacuzzi and pad over to the lounge.

Eschewal shuts his eyes as Tanisha kisses and rubs his chest. His penis hardens. *The Dog's* barking shatters his mind as if demanding to be released. He lifts his arms above his head. Tanisha pulls them around her neck. He lifts them again above his head. Tanisha pulls them around her waist. He lifts them again above his head.

Tanisha frowns, then slips her hand into his boxers. Before he can push her hand away, she has his penis. Up and down she goes; fast, then slow. She squeezes the tip as if trying to release his frustrations. He closes his eyes and leans back as he goes to war with *The Dog*. He thinks all he has to do is slide his hand down to her panties and pull them off, and then they will be having sex.

He licks his lips, remembering how good sex feels. *The Dog's* barking turns into a howl that must get the sexual gratification now.

He believes *The Dog's* urge has won. He says to himself, *"Alright, bruv, get ready to mash up some pum-pum."*

Then Tanisha says, "I hope you want this as I do?"

And just like that, *The Dog's* urge subsides. He pushes her hand away.

She says, "What's wrong?"

He replies, "Can love be bigger than sex? I mean, if you truly love something, can that thing stop you from indulging in casual sex?"

She does not answer.

He pushes himself out of the Jacuzzi. He can feel that power drawing through him. That power of being in love, whether it be achieving his dream or an individual devoting their life to religion in exchange for eternal life.

Chapter 36

NEXT DOOR IN THE lounge, Soshana flicks Deuce's hand away as he tries to guide his penis between the sides of her thongs.

"Oi, stop going on silly, man. I thought you were a big girl. So how you going on like you ain't done a one-night stand before?"

Soshana blushes and replies, "I am a big girl, and I have done one-night stands before, but that was before."

Deuce coughs hard, trying to hide his frustration. He shoots back, "So what are you saying, you won't do another one?"

She shrugs. "I don't know; it depends..."

He sucks his teeth. "Depends on what?"

She flicks her hair. "I don't know, the right time."

He huffs and shakes his head. He says to himself, *"I know what time it is. Please make it be fresh."* He kisses her neck. "I know what want, but I never ever do this." He thinks, *'Shit, I gotta do this finger test real quick.'* He slides down her body, kissing it on the way. He reaches her belly button and dips his tongue in and out of it while simultaneously pulling her thongs aside. He dips his index finger inside her vagina. He slides it in and out, making her juices flow.

He looks up.

Her eyes are closed.

He turns his head to the side and smells his finger. It smells fresh. He sucks his teeth, vexed because he hates having to give oral just to get sex, but when the sensation of *The Dog* rages, he will do anything to get his fix of sex.

He smiles. He gets up from his knees in the darkened room as he prepares to give her the consequences of having to give her oral before sex. He tells her to turn around, then, holding his penis, he rolls on his emergency condom. He plans on cursing Spiv about the unavailability of condoms in the hotel because now he can only do one round.

He grips her left shoulder, then rams forward and penetrates.

She screams as the pressure from behind bolts through her chest.

Chapter 37

IN THE BEDROOM WHERE Spiv has Yashima, Soshana's screams reach him. The sound alone gives him the experience of *The Dog* in him bursting out of its cage. His penis expands even more, and with the lights down low, he feels confident to make his move for sex. He looks over at Yashima. She is sprawled over on the bed.

He says to her, "You ready to give me some hairs?"

She says, "Boy, I don't know, I don't really get down on the first night, you know."

"Ter," says Spiv. He smiles over at her as his semi-hard-on deflates and says, "Why are you going on like that for?"

She does not answer.

He repeats, "Come on, man, why are you going on like that for? Is it because I ain't got on no condom?"

She nods.

He adds, "Just cool, man, you only live once, you know, because if you're gonna dead, you're gonna dead, it's just your time to go, you feel me?"

She still makes no reply, although she agrees with the last statement the condom was not the problem. She also went by the rule that any guy who wants to have sex with her has to give her oral first.

Spiv sucks his teeth and gets up, and walks towards the door. He pauses in his thoughts, then says, "Come here." He fans her towards him. "Listen to this."

She puts her ear to the bedroom door. The sounds

Dirty Dog

from the lounge have turned from screams to a wailing cry that does not reflect pain but an excitable pleasure.

Soshana is now used to the size and enjoying the pounding penetration.

Yashima swallows hard. Her nipples stiffen as she hears Soshana hollering, "Oh shit, you big dick… ah, your dick is so fucking big…"

Yashima turns around and hopes Spiv's penis will make her say the exact words that her cousin is screaming. She kisses his chest and grabs his buttocks.

He leads her over to the bed with a full erection.

She makes a grab for his penis.

He tries to pull away, but it is too late.

He grits his teeth and lets her hold it for a while, then slowly pulls away. He hopes she cannot tell the size of his penis.

He turns her around, gives her oral for a few minutes, then slips his penis into her vagina.

She encourages him with a few fake cries of enjoyment. She knows doing the penis measurement test is pointless, so she stays bent over until he stops sweating and ejaculates.

Chapter 38

THE COLD WINTER SUN creeps up in the sky as the guys find their way home.

Deuce smiles as Eschewal drives onto the high road that leads to their town. He grabs his crotch and then looks over at Eschewal. "Hey, cuz," he begins, "did you bang your one?"

Eschewal does not take his eyes off the road. He replies, "Nah, blood, long, I wasn't even feeling it."

With surprise, Deuce says, "What? Are you stupid? That fit, ting, you didn't kill it?" He looks over at Spiv, lounging in the back seat. "Oi, Spiv," says Deuce, "are you listening?"

Spiv has his eyes closed. "Yeah, go on," he replies without opening them.

Deuce laughs and points his thumb towards Eschewal. "Oi, you know my man never go thru on the ting, though. Ter, can you believe it that fit bloodclart, ting, he never go thru?" He pauses, then huffs. "He must've sucked her pussy, fam. You get me?" He laughs to himself at the last statement. He wishes it were true.

Spiv makes no reply and keeps his eyes closed.

Deuce looks back over at Eschewal, and with a smirk, he says, "Nah, fam, big and serious, fun and joke done, did you suck her pussy?"

Eschewal does not crack a smile; he says, "Hey, bruv, who you talking to, you cat? Oi, bruv, you're gassed, you know. Oi listen, mind how you talking, you know. How you gonna ask bad man them ting there?"

Deuce retorts, "Forget bout bad man. Did you suck her pussy?"

Eschewal shakes his head from side to side and changes down a gear, then replies, "Ter, hold on, you taking man for some fool? Man, don't suck pussy, star."

Deuce fires back, "So what, have you never sucked pussy?"

Eschewal looks over at Deuce with a contemptuous scowl. "You never hear what I just said; I don't suck pussy, blood." He puts his eyes back on the road and his mind on the time he went down and tasted *hell*. He looks back over at Deuce and feels like spitting. He would never confess to someone like Deuce. He shakes his head and puts his eyes back on the road.

Deuce knows Eschewal is lying and wishes he would not so he can get his secret out in the open. He leans back in the chair and sucks his teeth while Eschewal drives him and Spiv home.

Six Months Later

Chapter 39

ESCHEWAL AND DEUCE SIT in silence with music humming in the background. Deuce waits for any potential girls to walk past the car so that he can talk them into having sex with him later on in the night. Eschewal hopes to see the girl in the park, as he believes hanging out on street corners will raise his chances of seeing her. He has been doing this now for the past couple of months.

He looks out of his car window, and his stomach twists. He shakes his head. He has had enough. He wants to give up on his search for the girl in the park, but his heart will not let him. He feels like screaming. He looks over at Deuce. "Oi, rudeboy, there's nothing out here," he states with a frustrated tone.

Just before Deuce can retort, a sexy girl steps past the car. "Oh shit, look at that…"

Eschewal twists his head around and brings into view the girl's juicy, fat, plump backside.

Deuce says, "Rah, I'm gonna call her." He pops the door and springs out. "Oi, oi, oi," he hollers. "Oi, baby girl..."

The girl takes no notice of his cry because for one reason: her name is not, Oi. She keeps her head straight and wiggles her way up the road.

Deuce yells for her attention one last time, then gives up and spits abuse, "Cha, anyway, suck yourself. You're going on like you're nice like your shit don't stink." He jumps back in the car, his pride

Dirty Dog

dented. He sucks his teeth. "You see me, though, bruv, try go on like she's nice with her lean-up shoes." He again sucks his teeth.

Eschewal shakes his head and laughs.

Like an actor changing into roles, Deuce wipes the vexation from his face and dons a smile. He rolls the window fully down and gets ready to talk. "Hello, hello." He gets the attention of a young-looking girl wearing tight-fitted jeans and a low-cut top. She stops and turns towards the window.

"What's up pretty, wha gwan?"

The girl smiles and moves a bit closer.

Deuce sticks his hand out the window and shakes the girl's hand. "So what's your name then, pretty?"

"Nina," replies the girl.

Deuce nods. "Mmmm, Nina, yeah, you look good, though, innit, Nina? Can I get your number?"

Nina shakes her head. "Nah, I can't…"

"Why, have you got a boyfriend?"

"Yeah, I got a boyfriend, and he wouldn't be too happy with me chatting to next man, innit."

Deuce smirks. "Alright, babes. I'm not gonna hold you up any longer. I'm gonna let you go."

A slight disappointment flashes across Nina's face; she wants a bit more attention. She waves, turns on her heels, and says, "Bye."

Moments later, Deuce shrieks, "Oh shit… Look at them two chicks, blood."

"Where?" says Eschewal, bending his neck and trying to spot the girls.

"Over there, crossing the road."

Eschewal spots the two thick-body girls, both wearing short skirts.

"Come, man, let's jump out and call them," demands Deuce.

"Hold on, man, wait until they cross the road, man."

Von Mozan

Deuce sucks his teeth. "You're going on like you're frightened," then hops out of the car.

Eschewal stays seated and watches.

"Oi," bellows Deuce, getting the girls' attention just before they can swerve off to the right and walk down the main road. They look towards him; he waves them over. The girls grab each other by the arm and stroll towards Deuce with grins.

Chapter 40

THE GIRLS WANT TO work as fast as Deuce with the exchange of numbers and to set a time to meet. Eschewal gets out of the car and heads towards the corner shop.

Deuce gets the numbers from the girls and watches as they walk off, hoping to meet more guys with whom they can give their numbers and meet up for sex.

Eschewal is on his way back from the corner shop. He does not notice a pair of luscious legs behind him. Deuce spots them instantly; he indicates to Eschewal to stop the girl. Eschewal cannot hear what Deuce is saying and keeps stepping toward the car. He reaches it and opens the door.

Deuce yells and points. "Look, cuz. I was telling you to stop that, chick."

Eschewal looks around and catches the back view of the girl. He says, "So why didn't you jump out and stop her?"

Deuce sucks his teeth. "Because you were right near her, innit, you dick head." He pops the car door and chases the girl. He reaches the edge of the corner and hollers, "Hello, hello…"

The girl stops and turns around.

Deuce waves her to him.

She hesitates and squints her eyes as she tries to determine if she knows Deuce.

He waves again. "Come here, man."

Dirty Dog

The girl puts her hand on her hip and strolls up to him with her two shopping bags in her other hand.

Eschewal watches from the car as Deuce charms the girl. She smiles and nods. She smiles and nods again, then moves from the corner towards the car with Deuce leading.

Deuce gets to the car and says to Eschewal, "Oi, blood, you don't mind dropping this beautiful girl home, do you?"

Before Eschewal can reply, Deuce mouths, "We can link her later, and both go thru."

Eschewal wants to say, *"So what. I don't want a threesome. I just want to find the girl in the park,"* but he shrugs and says, "Yeah, whatever, I'll drop her."

Deuce gets in the front as the girl bundles in the back.

Eschewal drives off.

Chapter 41

AS ESCHEWAL DRIVES ALONG the high street, he passes scrolls of people walking and enjoying the summer evening.

He looks into his rearview mirror and the eyes of the girl. He catches a glimpse of her lustful, fiery sexual passion. He knew from this that Deuce had spoken the truth, and she would be up for a threesome.

Like bats out of hell, butterflies shoot into Eschewal's stomach as the imagery of *The Dog* arises within him, ready to pounce.

He thinks, *'Shit, how the hell am I gonna control The Dog in me after going without sex for one year?'* He smiles as he thinks he will let *The Dog* take over. *'At least, this way, my heart will not have a chance, and I will have to end my search when I do the threesome.'*

He pulls the car into a sharp right and shakes his head again as he reminisces on a sentence from the black book: *One needs the discipline to think. Then comes control.* He mumbles, "Yeah."

Deuce looks over at him. "Did you just say something, bruv?"

"Nah, nah," replies Eschewal as he flicks his nose.

Deuce spins around to face the girl and says loud enough so Eschewal can hear, "Oh, I thought you asked if this girl was adventurous." Deuce waits for Eschewal's reply hoping that he will follow his lead.

With a deep breath, Eschewal says, "Nah... why, is

she?"

Deuce grins. "Of course she is, ain't you, babes?"

The girl licks her lips. "Well, that's for me to know and for you lot to find out, innit."

Deuce loves when girls use that phrase; it always gets him aroused. "That's what I keep telling them, ter, she's cold," He punches Eschewal's knee, then says, "Can we link you later on and find out, then?"

"I don't know, um," begins the girl as she thinks about what time her so-called boyfriend (whom she hasn't seen for a month) promised he would come around. He told her nine o'clock, so she decides to give him an extra hour, and if he does not show up, she would go off with Deuce and Eschewal. She answers Deuce, "Yeah, maybe. Take my number and give me a call about ten o'clock."

Deuce nods with a perverted grin. "Yeah, go on. What's the number?"

She taps Eschewal's shoulder. "Yeah, babes, stop here." He stops the car outside a tall grey housing block.

She finishes giving Deuce her number. As she gets out of the car, Deuce leans over and slips his hand between her butt cheeks.

"Naughty," says the girl.

Deuce replies, "Listen, I'm gonna be even more naughty when I come for you."

She sticks out her tongue and swishes her head forward as Deuce says, "Oi, what's your name again?"

"Salacious," says the girl without turning back, leaving Deuce to watch her big bottom moving up and down as she walks to her housing block.

Chapter 42

DEUCE AND ESCHEWAL MAKE their way over to a wine bar to kill some time until ten o'clock. "Oh shit, she's fit," begins Deuce as Eschewal connects to the main road, "nah, blood serious, do you really know how fit that chick is?"

Eschewal nods in agreement. "That's what I keep telling them."

Deuce continues, "Ter, can you imagine how her body looks when you take off her clothes? I swear you due to buss a nut before you even push it in."

Eschewal shakes his head and laughs. "Yeah, true stories?" he says.

"Yeah, cuz," says Deuce, "but not me, 'cause I'm rolling with the fitness, blood. Trust me. I'm not bussing until I mash that down."

Eschewal smiles. "Yeah, better that boy," then rubs his head.

Silence falls between the two for a while, then sounding less scared but more concerned, Deuce says, "Oi, you don't think she'll back out, do you?"

Eschewal shrugs. "Boy, I don't know, bruv," he says, hoping she will not.

Deuce continues, "Nah, I don't think she's gonna back out. I'm telling you, bruv, every girl that I know are hoes, trust me. That's why I do what I do. Even though I love my wifey, I don't trust her. You feel me?"

Eschewal raises his eyebrows, not in agreement but

understanding Deuce's guilt-driven rationalization.

He pushes the car through the last set of traffic lights and drives past the wine bar. As he looks for a parking space, his memory replays the look of sexual need in Salacious's eyes. *"Yeah,"* he tells himself, *"she won't be backing out."*

Chapter 43

THE TIME IS FIFTEEN minutes to ten. Salacious has been arguing with her boyfriend for the past hour. Her battery has just died, so the argument is cut off, but the fight has not ended. She runs to the charger and plugs in her phone. With tears waiting to burst from her eyes, she waits until her boyfriend answers the phone.

"Yeah, so what are you saying?"

"You know what I'm saying," replies the boyfriend.

Her throat chokes up. "Yeah, but I don't understand why?"

He lowers his tone of voice, "You know why. I need some space. Like the relationship is going too deep too quick."

"What do you mean?" she cries. "We've been seeing each other for over six months. And I haven't even seen you for a month."

"Yeah, I know, but you've heard what I've said."

She sobs.

He overlooks her sobbing, then says, "Listen, I'm going to talk to you, I'm gonna talk to you soon, but I've gotta go. Later." He ends the call hoping he will have her psychologically weak for him.

He is successful. The mind game worked because even though Salacious is a gorgeous girl with a pleasant personality, she has low self-esteem. From a little girl, her mother told her, *"Why can't you tidy up your room and keep it clean? You know when you get big, you're never gonna be able to keep a man because no man don't want no nasty girl who can't clean."*

These taunts haunted Salacious, and whenever she had a boyfriend, she lived in fear that he would somehow see that untidy little girl in her.

She sits on the edge of her bed, holding her phone, as she continues to sob. She opens her phone to call back her boyfriend; when the phone rings, an unknown number flashes up. She wipes away the tears and answers, "Yeah, hello?"

"Yeah, hello, is this Salacious?"

"Yeah, who is this?"

"Ricky," lies Deuce. He continues, "Um, yeah, one of the dudes that dropped you off earlier."

Salacious' boyfriend's psychological hold momentarily falls away. She jumps into her sexy character voice, "Hi, what's up, babes? I didn't think you were gonna call."

"Course I was gonna call," replies Deuce. "So what you saying? Are you going to link, man?"

"Um... yeah, um, come and pick me up in about half an hour." She ends the call. She throws down her phone on the bed and runs to the bathroom to freshen up.

Chapter 44

DEUCE SLAPS ESCHEWAL ON his arm. "Oi, blood, she said we must pick her up in half an hour." Deuce grips his crotch. "Oh shit, we're woking tonight, blood."

Eschewal shows no emotion; he had misjudged his heart. It had beaten *The Dog* back into its cage. His heart will not let him give up on his dream. "Oi, bruv," he begins, "I'm gonna be real. I'm not even feeling it."

"Feeling, what?" says Deuce, sounding puzzled.

"Yeah, bruv, I'm not feeling this threesome ting. I'm not on it."

Deuce's voice almost chokes up, "Why?"

"This galist ting is getting long. I want a wifey as well," lies Eschewal. All he wants is a wife, namely the girl in the park.

Deuce sucks his teeth. "Having a wifey is long, you know. Ber headache, bruv. I wish I was like you, with no wifey."

Eschewal huffs and shakes his head. "Nah, trust me, bruv, I'm not on it. It's long."

Deuce's heart feels as if it has dropped out of his chest. He panics and says, "Oi, bruv, to find a wifey is hard, you know, and trust me, you will never find one if you go out looking." He screws his face and then continues, "That's what life is like, bruv. When you want something, you can't get it, and then once you get it you don't want it." He quickly pauses to see if he is beginning to sway Eschewal's decision. He continues as he points his finger. "Yeah, so you should just bang different chicks, bruv until you find the one."

Eschewal shakes his head, not knowing how to answer. He has to be careful not to blow his cover that he is no longer a player.

Deuce falls silent and changes tactic, "Alright, at least, let me bring her to your yard then?"

"Nah, bruv. Laow that, man. Laowit."

"Go on, man. Please, man. You know I would do it for you. Come, man, please."

Eschewal sucks his teeth and feels like cursing. "Alright, man, but this is the last time, you know."

Forty-five minutes later, Eschewal pulls up outside Salacious' housing block.

She comes out wearing tight jeans that are tucked into high-heeled boots and a waist-high jacket. She pauses for a few seconds, then taking two deep breaths, she sashays over to Eschewal's car.

Chapter 45

*F*OR THE PAST FIFTEEN minutes, Deuce has been trying to get Salacious next door in the bedroom.

"Nah, stop!" she says, leaning off Deuce's shoulder.

"Ah, babes, man, why you going on like that for?"

She pulls his hand from behind her. "Just give me some space, man."

He wants to suck his teeth and disrespect her, but instead, he smiles and whispers, "You need a drink before anything goes down, innit?"

She twiddles her hair. "I'm not saying that, but it would be nice to have a drink, yes."

He looks over at Eschewal and grins. "Oi, blood, I beg you a favor, go shop for me, please?"

For a moment, Eschewal does not respond or take his eyes off the TV. He slides his hands down his legs as he stretches them out. "Alright, give me the money then," he says with an even tone. He wants Deuce and Salacious out of his house as quickly as possible.

Deuce gets up. "Buy a half-a-bottle of brandy and a bottle of coke, yeah," he mouths, "and a box of condoms."

Eschewal nods. "Alright, man, I'll be back in a minute," he leaves the room.

Salacious looks at the time on her phone. She had hoped her boyfriend would have called back, deterring her from what she is about to do.

Under her breath, she says, "Bastard," then switches off her phone. She turns to Deuce close enough to kiss him and says, "Are you upset with me, babes?"

For a moment, he does not answer and wonders, *'Why do girls love to play games?'* He shakes his head and smiles. "Nah, I'm not upset, babes, but you're going on cold, innit?"

She licks her lips. "I just got something on my mind," she says while pushing her body onto him.

Instantly he gets an erection.

"Yeah, well, let me try and take that off your mind." He gropes her up and down.

She lifts her head, revealing her neck.

He bites down on it, and she moans.

He sucks and licks. She moans some more.

His hand wanders towards her crotch. He unzips her jeans halfway and says, "Oi, come, let's go next door to the bedroom?"

"Nah, I'm not ready." She zips up her jeans.

"What?" he responds, sounding confused and upset because *The Dog's* urge is upon him and needs to be unleashed.

"Nah, not yet," she pleads as she moves away.

He sucks his teeth. Thoughts of getting ruff with her come and go because Eschewal could come back at any minute.

Chapter 46

ESCHEWAL PULLS UP TO the kerb in front of his house. From out of nowhere, a vision hits him. He sees himself and Deuce having a threesome with Salacious. He shakes his head and switches off the engine.

As he picks up the blue plastic bag containing the half-a-bottle of brandy, a bottle of coke, and a box of condoms, the vision hits him harder. He grits his teeth and clicks open the door.

On jumping out of the car, his heart pounds in his chest as the vision becomes clearer. "Shit," he says as he shuts the door and locks the vehicle.

He blinks and focuses. He feels like swearing. He cannot believe that just one vision has released *The Dog*.

He waits a moment to see if his heart will respond… nothing. *The Dog* is loose.

His only hope is if Deuce has already had sex with Salacious because if he has not, then a threesome will be going down, drawing the search for the girl in the park to an end.

He approaches his front door as if treading in deep mud. He takes a second to think, *'This world is nuts. It seems as if it only gives you a beautiful wifey, who will love you and do everything for you, only if you plan to cheat on her twenty-four-seven.'*

He shakes his head, fits his key into the lock, and creeps into his own house.

Dirty Dog

He stops in the passage for a moment and listens to see if he can hear Deuce having sex with Salacious. He cannot hear any noises, so he closes the front door with a bang to ensure that if they are having sex, they are not anymore.

Chapter 47

ESCHEWAL ENTERS THE ROOM. He cannot tell if anything went down, but as he walks over to hand Deuce the blue plastic bag containing the half-a-bottle of brandy, a bottle of coke, and a box of condoms, he sniffs the air to make sure.

Deuce takes the bag. "Nice one, mate," he says, pulling out the half-a-bottle of brandy and bottle of coke from the blue plastic bag and stuffing the box of condoms that is still inside the bag down the side of the sofa. He opens the brandy and looks over at Eschewal, who is making his way over to sit down. "Oi, blood, do you want a drink?"

"Nah, I'm cool," replies Eschewal as he sits on the sofa.

Deuce picks up a glass from the coffee table in front of him and pours a large measurement of brandy.

Salacious says to Eschewal, "Don't you drink?"

He rubs his chin and shakes his head. "Nah, I don't drink."

She looks at Deuce. "You don't drink either?"

He pours a bit of coke into the glass of brandy. "Nah, babes, I don't really drink, but I'm gonna have a little glass. You get me?"

She smiles and rubs her hand down her leg. "Is it you lots plan to get me drunk and have your wicked way with me?"

In a smooth tone, Deuce replies, "Nah, babes. Don't say that. Nothing can't go on if you don't want it to go on. You feel me?" He offers her a glass of brandy and coke.

She smirks, making her full juicy lips twist. She takes the drink and sips. She licks her lips. "Ooh, too strong, do you wanna kill me? Nah, eya mix it a bit more."

He pours coke into the brandy until she tells him to stop.

She crosses her legs, smiles, then gulps the brandy and coke. She closes her eyes and bites her bottom lip. Her body feels heavy, as if the gravity force of a black hole is pulling her towards the floor.

Like a bolt of electricity, her mind sends a chill up and down her spine. Her nipples are erect. She gets up from the seat and puts down the glass of brandy and coke.

She says calmly and relaxed, "Alright, guys, when I get back from the bathroom. You two better be stripped naked and ready because I will be."

Eschewal looks at Deuce with an expression that says, *'Is she for real?'*

Deuce raises his eyebrows and shrugs.

Chapter 48

$\mathcal{S}$ALACIOUS HAS BEEN IN the bathroom for five minutes. Deuce gets an idea to go there after her and finish what he thought he was about to get before Eschewal came back.

Deuce jumps up from his seat and strides over to the door. He opens it and steps out, then quick as a flash, he steps back in. "Oh shit," he slips his right leg out of his jeans and throws it on the floor.

Eschewal's eyebrows scrunch together. "What you doing, blood?"

Deuce drags off his shirt. "What do you mean, what am I doing?"

Eschewal replies, "Why are you stripping off for?"

"Ter, sick, we're getting pussy tonight, gee." Deuce slips out the box of condoms from down the side of the sofa.

Eschewal makes no reply, for he now knows Deuce saw something in the hallway. What Deuce saw, not even he expected to see: the silky, smooth, sensuous firm body that lay beneath Salacious's clothes.

The door pushes open. In steps Salacious, with perky, erect breasts and wearing silky cream thongs.

The feeling of tiny fluttering butterflies, probably at the same time, swish around inside Deuce and Eschewal's stomachs. For them, it was rare to see a body like Salacious': small waist, a round juicy butt, and firm, supple breast.

With seductive eyes and curling her lips, she says to

Dirty Dog

Eschewal, "Aren't you getting undressed?"

Before he can answer, Deuce pulls off his vest, and as he leads Salacious out of the room, he turns to Eschewal and says, "Ter, sick..."

Chapter 49

ESCHEWAL IS LEFT IN the living room with a full erection and the sounds of *The Dog's* howls reverberating in his head.

In his mind's eye, he sees the face of the girl in the park and remembers how she made him feel. The feeling was beyond lust. It consumed him and took his breath away. The feeling could only be love, a love, which is the strongest emotion a human can feel. A love that he has begun to believe he would never be allowed to have.

It seemed as if he had blinked his eyes after that last thought, and when he reopened them, he found himself standing in the bedroom in his boxer shorts, looking down at Salacious. He had hoped before now the girl in the park would have saved him from *The Dog's* urges: he was wrong.

Deuce turns his head to him. "Oi, bruv," he begins as he lifts Salacious' right leg, exposing her vagina, "have you ever seen anything like this? Look how good it looks, bruv."

At the exact moment that Eschewal looks at Salacious' pretty vagina, he destroys the mental image of the girl in the park.

The search is finally over. The goal not to have sex again until he finds the girl in the park crumbles away as he pulls off his boxers and slips on a condom.

Three Months Later

Chapter 50

ESCHEWAL AND DEUCE SIT in a wine bar. Eschewal's face is subdued. He cannot believe the search for the girl in the park is over. He was so sure she was made for him. He sips on his glass of orange juice and looks over at Deuce. For over a year, since Eschewal decided hanging out with Deuce was a good idea to find the girl in the park, Deuce had hooked him up with over fifty girls. Eschewal had dodged having sex with everyone except Salacious.

The feeling of wasted time makes him feel sick. He looks away from Deuce. He has made his mind up. He will waste no more time and will not let *The Dog* take over his life. The first female who catches his eye, he will make her his wife; his one and only.

Deuce turns to him. "Oi, blood, it looks like there's gonna be ber, young tings in here tonight, blood."

Deuce is right; there will be a new set of young females fresh out of college ready to enjoy the freedom of weekend raving.

Eschewal nods then smirks as he would not mind a young female that he could groom. He sips his juice, then says, "Yeah, it looks like it, innit."

Deuce leans back in his chair, excited that he has his right-hand man back with him, setting out on another rampage, unaware Eschewal has other plans.

Eschewal twists his head slightly to the left, and his eyes bring into view a young female by the bar. He studies her for a bit and takes notice of her straight white teeth, beautiful slender hands, and feet.

He imagines himself marrying the girl and making sweet love to her. The vision blurs with the image of the girl in the park. He huffs and mumbles, "That dream is over. The dream is dead."

He springs up from his seat and slides over to the bar where the girl stands.

Deuce takes a sip of his drink and watches with envy as the girl gives Eschewal her number.

Chapter 51

THE CAR GLIDES THROUGH the night streets. Music plays in the background. Eschewal slows the car down as he approaches a roundabout and indicates to go right.

"Nah, blood, take the left," says Deuce. "I'm hungry, blood. What aren't you hungry?"

"Yeah, I'm kind of hungry still," says Eschewal as he stirs the car left and moves down the road towards an all-night fast-food take-away.

Deuce flicks his fingers towards Eschewal and says, "Oi, bruv, did you get that chick's number?"

Eschewal plays the fool. "Which chick?"

"The chick back at the bar, man. The fit ugly, ting."

Eschewal kisses his teeth and then replies, "She ain't ugly. Why you hating for? Don't hate. The girl is abstract, man."

Deuce rolls his eyes. "Forget about that, the bitch is ugly, man, but she's rarseclart fit. She's fit till I feel sick. Did you get the number, then?"

Eschewal pulls the car to the kerb in front of the take-away. His player dialogue rolls out, "Course, man, I don't ramp, you know."

He picks his phone up off the dash and flicks through his contact numbers to check if he has stored the number.

Deuce asks, "What's her name?"

"She calls herself Peachy."

"Is that her real name?"

Dirty Dog

"That's what she said, gee." Eschewal throws the phone back on the dash, not realizing what is about to happen to him.

Deuce dips into his pocket. "Ah, bruv, listen, I'm tired, you know. I beg you get the food for me, please."

Eschewal nods and takes Deuce's money. He jumps out of the car.

Deuce picks up Eschewal's phone. He plans to take Peachy from Eschewal because she glanced at him back at the bar. At that moment, seeing the lust in her eyes, he knows she will be his. Smiling, he steals her number.

Three Days Later

Chapter 52

ESCHEWAL REACHES FOR THE TV remote as the latest top comedy show ends. He flicks through the other channels and finds nothing to watch. The next suitable show will not be starting until the next hour. He throws down the remote on the stylish coffee table and rests back into his leather sofa. He stares up at the ceiling. He sighs then shakes his head. He closes and rubs his eyelids, then opens them and continues to stare at the ceiling. He thinks about what to do now to kill some time. He smiles as he recalls the phrase: *You do not kill time. Time kills you.*

He sits up and looks over at his phone, and for a few seconds, he does nothing. Then as if he has received an electric shock, he jumps toward his phone. He remembers that he has not yet called Peachy.

He scrolls down to her name and resumes a calm composure. He moves over to his CD player and turns on some music. He taps the call button and sends a dialing tone to her phone. He sits down as it rings. A second later, she answers.

"Yeah, hello," he begins as he swallows hard, trying to control his nerves. "Is this, um, Peachy?"

"Yeah," she says, "who is this?"

He relaxes further into the seat as her welcoming tone puts him at ease.

"Oh, what's up, babes? This is um, Eros… we met at the bar last week."

She laughs, a cute laugh, and says, "Oh yeah, are you all right? What are you up to?"

He replies, "Um, um, just chilling, babes. What are you saying? When will we set a date to get to know each other better?"

"I don't know. It's up to you."

He grins that she responds positively and does not lead the conversation on for too long because he has not got much credit left on his phone.

In a confident tone, he suggests a movie on Friday at eight.

She agrees.

He ends the conversation with a sweet compliment.

She smiles, chuckles, then says bye.

He ends the call, and as his thoughts drift off, he wonders, *'Is she the one?'*

Chapter 53

SITTING IN HIS CAR, moments later, Deuce dials Peachy's number. He turns down the music from the radio, as she answers her phone.

"Yeah, hello," he says, "is this ah, Peachy?"

With suspicion in her voice, she says, "Yeah… who is this?"

Deuce clears his throat. "Yeah, um, this is Ricky."

A moment of silence passes as she waits for him to continue.

"I don't know if you will remember me, but you gave me your number a few months ago at that bar on the high road."

She is about to hang up because the only time she has ever been to that bar on the high road was when she met Eschewal, and that was three days ago. However, the excitement of discovering who this mystery caller is makes her stay on the line.

With a little giggle, she says, "Is it? Are you sure I gave you my number? Because I hardly ever give it out."

"Course, I'm sure," he begins, "how else did I get your number then?"

She giggles once again. "That's what I want to find out. What did you say your name was again?"

He swallows. "Ricky," he pauses, then describes himself. "Don't you remember me? I'm like well-built, short hair and dimples."

She licks her lips as the description resembles the

Dirty Dog

guy she saw with Eschewal. She shakes her head and says, "You know what, I don't remember you. This is a wind-up, innit?"

He coughs, then panics. He knows if he says the wrong thing, he will lose the chance of meeting her. He decides to be upfront and tell her the truth.

"Alright," he begins, "I'm gonna be real with you. I saw you at that bar three days ago, and you gave your number to my friend, who had on the blue cap. Well, I thought you were so criss I stole your number out of his phone, and boy, I wanna link you."

She becomes light-headed. She had wished that Deuce had spoken to her instead. She makes no resistance as he suggests they meet within the next hour.

He grins. The steal went down easier than he thought. He grips his phone. *'Why are these chicks so stupid?'* He begins to himself. He continues, *'They always want the best-looking dudes, the shotters, or the baddest boy on the block but can never handle the harsh consequences.'* He shakes his head. *'Stupid bitches. Always looking surprised when they find out they got played.'* He huffs, *'What do they expect when they link a pretty boy like me?'* He looks into his rearview mirror, slides his tongue over his teeth, and says, "Yes, sweet boy, just another hoe."

He puts the car into gear, heading off to destroy and demoralize, with his lies and dishonesty, another female soul.

Chapter 54

DEUCE RESTS HIS BACK against the headboard. Peachy is in the bathroom. She steps back into the room, ready for sexual intercourse. She sits beside him in an S shape, curls her lips, and says, "I don't know. I feel bad linking you now after I talked to your friend and gave him my number."

He flicks his nose and replies, "Don't feel bad, babes. You did the right thing, trust me. Like he is my brethren, but you listening, he's a dirty dog. You feel me? He's all got a wifey, so you know he's not gonna take you seriously."

He looks down at her. He strokes her hair and stares into her eyes. "Nah, dem boy dere don't deserve a beautiful girl like you. You're too good for him, trust me."

She smiles. She wants to believe what he is telling her so she can justify her motives. She leans off her elbows, brings her body to the edge of the bed, and says, "Haven't you got a girl? Because you know what they say; birds of a feather flock together."

Without cracking a smile, he hits her with the twisted truth, "Yeah, I'm gonna be real. I have got a girl, but it's not working out. I've already told her I want to end it, but she's still clinging on, and right about now, I wanna get to know you. Upfront, I'm not saying that I wanna jump into a relationship with you right away, but I want to do a ting with you and just go with the flow."

Von Mozan

For a moment, Peachy remains quiet as she dwells on the information she has been fed. The information contains elements of honesty and hope, enough to convince her need for justification that Deuce could be the one she has been waiting for all her life.

He brings her away from her thoughts as he says, "So, babes, you wanna go with the flow and see how it goes?"

She licks her lips, shrugs, and says, "Yeah, alright then, I'm down with that."

For the next hour, he delivers foreplay until he gets her comfortable enough to give him sex.

Chapter 55

THE BIG DAY ARRIVES. Eschewal has been looking forward to his date with Peachy and is glad the working week has ended.

He dips his head underneath the bath water, resurfaces, and soaps himself up. He sinks his soaped-up body back into the water and then rinses off under the shower. His body, now feeling fresh and clean, he brushes his teeth.

He walks into his bedroom with a towel wrapped around his waist. He creams himself down with body lotion. He starts from his face to his feet.

He turns up the volume on the music. He gives a dance with a wiggle, and a turn, then stops. He picks up the roll-on deodorant and rolls it under his armpits, then between the inside of his thighs. He picks up the spray deodorant and sprays every nook and cranny. He steps back. Looking at the expensive cologne, he wonders which one of the six bottles he should wear tonight. He decides to wear the one that makes him smell sweet but not that sweet for it to be mistaken for perfume. He lays the sweet scent across his chest in a crisscross motion, then over his head. He pads over to his bed, where his dry-cleaned outfit is laid out and sprays it with the sweet scent.

He has finished grooming himself to the sweet-boy standard, and the only thing left to do is put on his clothes. He looks over at himself in the mirror. He sees his trapped image staring back at him, longing to

Dirty Dog

experience a life of happiness.

He speaks to his image and says, "As long as I can see you, then I know I still can become happy."

The image makes no reply. It seems to reflect a sense that it understands.

He turns away and puts on his clothes.

Ready to go, he looks at the time. He has half an hour to pick up Peachy and half an hour to get to the cinema. He decides to give Peachy a call and let her know he is on his way. He activates the number; he puts the phone to his ear and smiles, ready to reflect the smile in his voice. The smile disappears from his face as the phone rings out.

His heart sinks at the reality of what might be happening: that Peachy is listening to the phone ring and not answering it because it has his number flashing on the screen.

He shrugs off those negative feelings and tells himself, *"Maybe she's just running late, and she's still in the bathroom or something."*

He calls the number back. It rings twice then cuts itself off. He grips the phone and sits down.

He can feel his rage rising inside him. He is fuming at the probable reality but more fuming because he got all spruced up with nowhere to go.

Chapter 56

PEACHY SITS IN HER bedroom alone, hoping Eschewal gets the message and does not call back. She decides to call Deuce to ask if they can meet up. He lies and tells her he will call her back in five minutes.

Ten minutes pass, and with anxiety etched across her face, she is about to call him back when a withheld number flashes up on her screen. Without thinking, she answers, expecting to hear the voice of Deuce. Instead, she hears the voice of Eschewal.

The reality of what she has been doing, avoiding his call, hits Eschewal between his chest plates and makes him feel weak.

He controls his rage, and in a smooth tone, he says, "Are we still linking up?"

Peachy clears her throat and feels like all the blood in her body has drained to her legs as she prepares to lie. "Oh, I'm so sorry, babes, something has come up, so I can't make it."

He grits his teeth as a lump appears in his throat. He replies, "So you couldn't call from before and let me know?"

She slips out of the question, "Nah, because I just found out now, innit."

He once again calms the rage from exploding over her lies and says, as firmly as a president declaring war: "This thing that has come up, exactly what is it?"

"It's just something, innit," she hesitates, then adds, "I just got to do something."

With the first trace of anger in his voice, he retorts, "That's what I want to know. What have you got to do?"

She stays silent as her mind goes blank from trying to make up a good enough reason.

"Oi, are you listening?"

She remains silent.

This makes his voice rise higher with anger; he cannot control his emotion. "That's why I know you're an idiot; you can't even answer, man."

He grips the phone. His body shaking with anger, he wants to curse her out and say, *"Oi, when I see you, I'm gonna lick you over and buss-up your face. Respect something, you fucking butters."* But the thought disappears as he knows that thug inside him died long ago.

He ends the call, throws his phone on the table, and then sits down. The anger hasn't entirely left his body when his phone rings. He jumps up, thinking its Peachy. Instead, it is Deuce inviting him to a rave.

Eschewal takes a moment to decide. The repetitiveness of going out to raves and events so that he could see the girl in the park has taken its toll on him. Before, he had a purpose. Now it just seems there is no need, but reluctantly he agrees. After all, he is spruced up, and at least now he has somewhere to go.

Chapter 57

THE RAVE IS PACKED with females, but as they walk past Eschewal, he takes no notice of them. He no longer has the energy to look; he spent a year looking for that girl in the park and nothing.

He closes his eyes, and not thinking with a clear state of mind, he says to himself, *'Maybe Deuce is right; I should stop looking and just bang different chicks until I find the one. I think it's time to let The Dog run wild.'*

He has given up hope of finding a wife and becoming happy. He will let *The Dog* take over from here. He opens his eyes so *The Dog* can be set free to pounce. Two females swoop past him. His eyes become gripped on the one behind. He mumbles, "Rah, she's pretty." A moment passes, and his subconscious sends alarm bells to his memory. His legs feel as if a young Mike Tyson's fist has pounded them. His mouth falls open. He cannot believe it! He is looking at the girl in the park!

His feet seem stuck to the ground as his insides shoot an array of emotions, leaving his arms feeling like his legs and his fingers tingling.

His heart flutters. He bites his lip and wishes he never had sex but had held out as planned. It would have made this moment ever so perfect.

A smile spreads across his face as he realizes not everything in life can be perfect, and for the first time, he truly feels happy to be alive.

He has finally found her and is not going to lose her

again.

He looks over at Deuce and says, "Oi, I'll be back in a minute," then steps down the stairs to meet his princess.

Chapter 58

ESCHEWAL ENTERS THE DOWNSTAIRS bar area. He stops and looks around. His heart rate has fallen to normal but is on its way back up. He thinks for a moment that he has lost the girl again. Then finally, his eyes fall upon her. She stands by the bar, her beauty glowing and captivating him.

He smiles. *'What a life,'* he thinks, *'just when I gave up hope and least expected it, she steps back into my life.'*

He takes a deep breath; all his nerves have disappeared. He feels calm and confident. He borrows a pen from a guy who has written down his number 12 times and given it to 12 different girls. He writes down his number and begins his approach. He reaches the girl, grips her wrist, and leans in, then says, "If you want to find out how a real man treats a woman, give me a call."

She smiles, and his breath is taken away on seeing her beautiful teeth. He slides her his number, but before he leaves, he says, "Sorry, where's my manners. Would you like a drink?"

Once again, the girl reveals her beautiful teeth. She shakes her head and says, "No, thank you."

He nods. "Okay, I'll wait for your call then."

Cool as possible, he walks back out of the girls' life, wondering whether he has done enough to become a part of her life. Only time will tell.

"Yeah, only time will tell," he says to himself while walking back up the stairs.

Von Mozan

His last thoughts before reaching Deuce are, *'Was it a mistake not to ask for her name? Nah,'* he thinks, *'if it's not meant to be, I only want to remember her as THE GIRL IN THE PARK.'*

Three Days Later

Chapter 59

*N*IGHT HAS FALLEN. SALACIOUS has company inside her low-ceilinged, wide-windowed flat. She walks from the kitchen back into the living room with drinks.

"Are you gonna tell me the secret you've been hiding for the past two months, or what?"

"Hold your horses. I'm about to tell you now, innit. Eya," Salacious hands a drink over to her guest. She sits down, crosses her legs, and begins, "Well, you remember when we talked about our fantasy?"

"Yeah," replies her guest with excitement in her voice.

"Well…" Salacious bites her lip, "I did it…"

"Did what?" asks her guest because she remembers talking about three different fantasies.

"You know…" Salacious sticks two fingers in the air. "Two guys."

The guest screams, "You little tart," she covers her mouth and then says, "Oh my God, tell me everything. How was it?"

"I don't remember much of it, but you remember how I'm always complaining that I've never been satisfied? Well, that all changed." She giggles; you cannot tell whether it is from nerves or embarrassment.

The guest puts her hand over her mouth again. "I can't believe you did it. How do you feel now?"

Salacious shrugs. "I dunno, the same, but you know

Dirty Dog

I don't feel dirty or anything cause at the end of the day, they didn't fuck me. They fucked the condom."

She takes a sip of her drink and is about to continue. The guest butts in with, "So, who are these guys?"

Salacious shakes her head. "I don't know. I'm really bad." She laughs and continues, "The one who spoke to me first is called Ricky. He offered me a lift home, and I said yes, and then gave him my number. He called me later on that night, then I met him with his friend and went back to his friend's flat." She takes two sips of her drink and then continues, "I wasn't even going to go, but that bastard began messing around again, so I just said what the hell and went."

The guest laughs. "You're terrible." With a hint of sadness, she puts down her drink and adds, "I told Peen yesterday we can never get back together."

Salacious stays quiet. She loves her friend to the extent that they tell everyone they are cousins, and for ages, she has heard her friend say, "That's it, me and Peen are over." Only to discover that a few days later, they are back together and going through the same drama: him beating on her because she found out (again) that he had been cheating on her.

The guest picks up her drink. She knows what Salacious is thinking. "Nah, listen," the guest takes a sip, "I'm serious this time. I even took this guy's number at that rave I went to at the weekend, and I'm gonna call him now."

Salacious smiles. "Yeah, who is he? Where's he from?"

"I don't know, he gave me one cheesy line, but he was so sweet," replies the guest, taking out her phone and dialing the number.

Chapter 60

ESCHEWAL IS IN HIS living room, talking with a close friend. They are discussing life as a call comes through.

"Yeah, hello. Who's this?" says Eschewal. He pauses for a second, then looks at his friend. He does not believe that he just heard what he heard. "Sorry, say that again."

"It's the girl you gave your number to at the club on Saturday, don't you remember me?"

Again Eschewal pauses in silence. The first emotion to hit him makes him feel like stripping off his clothes and running down the road naked, screaming his excitement.

"Yeah, of course," he answers, controlling his joy. "So, anyway, I didn't get your name."

With a hint of amusement and seduction, the girl replies, "Oh, it's Manna."

He does not know it yet, but the name Manna will ring in his subconscious for many years to come. "Okay, is that like 'da manna?' Or does your name mean something else?"

A few seconds pass. Eschewal pulls the phone away from his ear, then puts it back. "Yeah, hello-hello." The call cuts off. He feels like throwing the phone on the wall. He believes that Manna might think he hung up the phone on her. He grits his teeth, worrying that she will not call back and because she withheld her number, he cannot call her back.

He sits there for a while, staring at his phone. His friend asks, "What's up, bruv, everything cool?"

Eschewal swallows the lump in his throat. "Yeah, man."

"Who was that on the phone?" says the friend.

Eschewal almost whispers, "Ah, no one, man," as he ends his sentence, his phone rings. He looks at the display; a number he does not recognize flashes up. His heart seems to scream out; this must be her, your princess; this was meant to be.

"Yeah, hello," his voice shoots down the phone with haste.

"Yeah, it's me. Sorry about that, babes, my battery died."

Eschewal lays back on his sofa and replies with a smile, "Nah, that's cool, babes. So what were you saying?"

And what Manna had to say led to a three-hour conversation. By the end, Eschewal had discovered almost everything about her life and vice versa. The conversation ended with a date set for the weekend, and that night when Eschewal went to bed, he did not sleep.

The Weekend

Chapter 61

ESCHEWAL IS STRESSING; HE has a problem: his car is still in the garage and will not be ready until tomorrow. He paces the living room holding his phone, wondering what to do. He knows this is the big test. Will Manna pull out of the date because there is no car, or will she prove to be the real woman of his dreams?

He takes a deep breath and calls her. "Yeah, hello. Is this Manna? Yeah, hello, yeah, it's me, Eschewal... Yeah, what's up, babes? Oi, listen, my car is in the garage."

He is about to explain that he will not get the car back until tomorrow when Manna butts in with, "Nah, that's cool, babes, I'll take a bus and come and meet you."

At that moment, he wants to bend down on one knee and propose marriage as he feels love strike at his heart.

"Eschewal, are you there?" she says.

He feels like he is about to shed tears. He swallows hard, then clears his throat. "Yeah, yeah, so you know how to get to the cinema then?"

She giggles. She can tell that he is shocked by her response. "Yeah, babes, I know where it is. I'll meet you outside there at eight."

"Okay, bye." he ends the call and stares at the floor. He feels it is too good to be true; a girl who looks as good as Manna is not superficial. A smile stretches

Dirty Dog

across his face as he enjoys the happiness that runs through his body.

He snaps out of his trance and heads off to groom himself to the sweet-boy standard.

Chapter 62

THE BUS, WHICH ESCHEWAL is on, shoots up the hill towards the cinema. He sits at the front of the double-decker bus, looking out the window. His thoughts run wild. He thinks, *'Why couldn't payday be this week? I would have sent a cab to pick her up. She's gonna think I'm Joe-Pinch-Penny, but what can I do? I'm about to spend all my money, which is my lunch money, for the rest of the week. Damn, I'm gonna have to eat buttered bread for the week and drink water from the office vending machine.'*

His palms sweat. His insecurities kick in. He tells himself that maybe Manna will not turn up. *'She's too good for me.'* he tells himself, *'I don't deserve someone like her. People like me aren't allowed happiness. I don't deserve her.'*

He feels like getting off the bus and going home. Before he acts, words from the black book come to mind; it reminds him: *I am a producer of values and no longer a destroyer of values, and that is where true self-esteem grows. But to keep it growing, I must never return to being a destroyer of values.*

He feels good about himself; he has done more good than bad and will continue doing good.

The bus pulls up at the cinema. He feels a numbing pain in his legs, and with his heart beating fast, he steps down the stairs.

He bounces off the bus. Manna sits poised on the bus bench. His heart melts as her beauty feels like it is suffocating him.

He plays it cool, then remembers to breathe. "Oh, I'm not late, am I?" he asks with a cheeky grin.

She looks at her watch. "No, I'm early," she says with a big smile as she gets off the bench.

He leads her to the cinema entrance. As they step through the doors and to the ticket office, then buy popcorn, he hopes she has not noticed that he has not taken his eyes off her. He wants to fall into her wide seductive eyes. He does not know who is more fortunate, him or her. He is going to love her like she never knew love before.

For the first time, as the film begins, he reaches out and takes hold of a woman's hand in public. He feels electricity run through his body. He looks at her. He rubs her hand, and they exchange smiles, then turn their heads back towards the film.

Chapter 63

THE NIGHT AIR IS cool, even though it is the start of winter.

The usual busy main road has only a few cars shooting up and down. Eschewal leads Manna towards the street crossing; they cross over to the other side of the road and stroll in the direction of the bus stops.

He calculates how much money he has left; it is enough to drop her home in a cab. The couple approaches the strip of road where the bus stops, cab station, and food outlets are clustered.

Eschewal contemplates what to do, *'Escort her home in a cab then walk back home or simply invite her back to my flat and work from there.'*

The pair speak at the same time. Eschewal ends his sentence, "…something to eat?"

"Yeah, I am a bit hungry."

He says to himself, *'Damn, why am I fronting. I don't have enough money to buy food.'*

His chest tightens up as if he is being restrained in a straitjacket. His only option is his credit card, which is almost maxed out.

He finally replies, "Okay, let's get something to eat. What do you feel for, pizza?"

"Yeah, I don't mind."

He and Manna head towards the pizza restaurant, but it has already closed. Once again, his chest tightens. He was looking forward to spending more

Dirty Dog

time with Manna. He looks over at the takeaway. He cannot see her coming home with him on the first date to eat a takeaway. However, his heart says something different.

"Would you like to get a takeaway and come back to mine?" he asks, almost holding his breath.

She smiles. "Yeah, why not?"

The tension runs out of his body as his eyes widen, and a huge smile appears. He leads her to the takeaway, then in a cab to his flat.

Chapter 64

THE LIGHTS ARE DOWN low. Eschewal and Manna have plates of food on their laps. They sit and eat in comfortable silence, with soft music humming in the background.

He cannot remember Chinese food ever tasting this good. Manna's aura makes every spoonful he eats taste sweeter and more delicious.

They finish eating and talk for the next two hours. Then, as casually as possible, Manna slips into Eschewal's arms.

He grows an instant erection, but not one full of lust that would make him want to start having sex. It is evenly balanced out with deep resonating love.

For the first time in so many years, his heart is overflowing with happiness, and he owes it all to Manna.

He smiles as he feels there is no longer the need to become a creator of values as he has all the happiness he needs.

He looks down and watches Manna fall asleep in his arms.

Chapter 65

IT IS A CHILLY sunny Monday morning, and Manna sits at her desk with a grin on her face. She cannot stop thinking about the other night she spent with Eschewal. She wonders why he had not tried to have sex with her. After all, she did end up in his bed, wearing only her underwear. It was the first time she had allowed herself to be in that position with a man, and he had not tried to have sex with her.

All night long, Eschewal had only held her in his arms, even though his penis was rock hard almost the whole night. This made such an impression that she was falling for him. This emotion puts a smile on her face.

She feels like phoning him to hear his voice. At that exact moment, her phone rings. She digs down into her purse. Her heart flutters as she wonders if it is Eschewal.

The name on the phone flashes up Spiv.

She answers it with joy in her voice, "Hi ya, babes."

"Yeah, what you saying?" responds Spiv.

"Nothing, I'm just at work, innit."

"So, how you sound so happy?"

She pauses and wonders if she should tell Spiv about Eschewal. *'Yeah, I might as well,'* she thinks. "Nah, it's nothing. It's just that I've met someone."

There is a sudden silence as jealousy runs down Spiv's spine. He thinks, *'After all the work I put in with her, now some fool is going to mess that up?'*

He plays it cool, controls his vexation, and makes Manna feel that he is happy for her. "Is it, don't lie?" he begins with fake excitement in his voice, "where did you meet him?"

"Um, last week Saturday at your club night."

Spiv searches his memory bank on who was there. There were so many players. "Okay, so what's his name?"

"Eschewal… Why, do you know him?"

"Nah, nah," he replies. He considers asking what Eschewal looks like but instead changes the subject.

When Spiv gets off the phone, he begins his investigation on Eschewal. There is no way he will lose out on time invested in being friends with Manna so he can get into her panties.

Chapter 66

THE CHILLY SUNNY MORNING ended and brought a cold-fresh-crisp night and a full moon shining high in the sky.

Deuce is on his way to Eschewal's house; he has a new girl for him and Eschewal. The girl has dreams of her and Deuce being lovers, but he has other ideas.

He pulls up two streets away from Eschewal's house and dials his number.

Eschewal answers.

Deuce begins his pitch, "Yes, blood, what you saying…? Hey, I've got a big link for me and you, blood. One sexy chick, she's on it."

In a blunt tone, Eschewal says, "Nah, bro, I'm not on it."

Deuce feels the muscles in his chest tighten up. He desperately needs Eschewal to drive him to meet this new girl because last week, his girlfriend's sister spotted him kissing another girl as she stepped out of his car. That night when he went home, his main argument was, *"Nah, babes, the girl is my workmate, and I didn't kiss her, she kissed me, and it was only a friendly kiss on the cheek after I dropped her to the bus stop."*

His girlfriend was not convinced, and Deuce knew he could not risk having girls in his car again.

He bites down on his lip as he controls his desperation from showing in his voice, then says, "Why are you not on it, blood?"

Eschewal feels a sinking sensation in his stomach.

Dirty Dog

He says, "I've met my wifey, blood. I'm telling you she's the one."

Deuce shrieks, "How you mean, she's the one? Listen, you can't just trust no girl. I told you before every girl that I know are cheating bitches. I'm telling you, that's why I do what I do."

Eschewal almost sucks his teeth as he says, "Bruv, I'm not watching that. If she wants to cheat on me, that's up to her. But I will never cheat on her, and that's real."

"So what you saying, you're not gonna come on this link?"

Eschewal shakes his head, not caring that he has now revealed he is no longer a player, and says, "Nah, I've told you, bruv. I've met my wifey. It's long."

Hate, spite, and madness twist in Deuce's throat. He can hardly get the words out, "Alright, blood, alright. I'll talk to you later." He squeezes his phone. He feels like smashing it on the window screen. *"Cunt,"* he says to himself, *"after all the links I brought him on, he was just trying to find a wifey? Liberties."* He leans back in his seat and stares out the window as he thinks of a way to get back at Eschewal.

Chapter 67

*S*PIV HAS JUST STEPPED into his house. He has been trying all day to get through to Deuce. At last, he gets a ringing tone.

Deuce's phone vibrates in his pocket. He lets it ring for a while, then without removing his stare, he uses his earpiece and answers the call. "Yeah, hello... who this...? Who?"

"Me, blood, man, Spiv. You going on like you don't know man's voice, what's wrong with you?"

Deuce coughs. "Nothing, man, I'm just chilling. What's going on?" Deuce wonders if he should bring Spiv to meet the girl. He decides not to because Spiv loves to show off his wealth around girls to make Deuce look small.

Spiv lowers his voice before he speaks, "Oi, cuz, you listening?"

"Yeah, go on," replies Deuce.

"Oi, do you know someone called, Eschewal?"

Deuce thinks for a moment, then says, "Nah, nah, why?"

Spiv sucks his teeth. "Listen, you know my ting, Manna? You know, she just told me that she linked some yute last week at my rave. You know I'm mad for that."

Deuce does not care; he has his own problems to deal with but pretends he does and says, "Yeah, rah, that's nuts, boy."

"I know, bruv, I need to find out who this yute is,

star. I can't make him take away this chick. I've been on her too long. You get me?"

"Yeah," replies Deuce, "I know how you feel, bruv, but forget about that. You know rarseclart Eros try say he's found a wifey and linking's long. After all the bloodclart links, I brought the yute on." He wipes the corners of his mouth, then continues, "Imagine that, when we were skinning out that link, he wasn't chatting that shit. Dick head, flipping dick head."

Spiv's attention is brought back into the conversation; he had zoned out for a while. He did not give a damn about Deuce's problem with Eschewal. He wanted to know why he was not aware of this threesome until now. "Which ting is this? What's her name?" says Spiv.

"Some, ting, innit. Rah, what's her name again…? Oh yeah, Salacious."

"Salacious," Spiv pauses, "um, where she come from?"

"From the ends, innit."

"Yeah, what does she look like?"

Deuce sucks his teeth. "Some pretty ting, fit, nice. Why?"

"Because you know who I think that is? That's rarseclart Manna's cousin. Trust me, that's Manna's cousin."

"Don't lie? Rah boy, me and Eros bun her boy, mash her down."

"Yeah, better that. Anyway, I'm gonna go. I have to call around and find out who this yute is. So are you sure you don't know who he is?"

"What's his name again?" says Deuce.

"Eschewal…"

Deuce pauses for a moment, "Eschewal… um, what does he look like?"

"I don't even know," replies Spiv.

Dirty Dog

"Where's he from?"

"I don't know, cuz he must be from the ends."

"Oi, hold on," begins Deuce as his memory of Eschewal's history returns to him.

"Isn't Eros's name a pet name?"

Spiv shakes his head. "Ah, I don't even know."

"Yeah, bruv, I remember now. Eros's real name is Eschewal." A sinister look crosses Deuce's face. "Yeah, you know, I totally forgot; true say everyone has always called him Eros. And trust me, I'm sure he is the only Eschewal on the ends."

Spiv has lost his breath for a while but now has it back. "Yeah, and the little pussyhole was at the club last week, innit? It must be him."

"It's him, bruv. He's taking the piss. Listen, just ask Manna, yeah, if this yute is also called Eros. Then just break his legs and tell her about Salacious, no long ting."

Spiv's eyes light up. "It's true, alright, brother, safe. I'm gonna give you a ring back, peace."

Chapter 68

SPIV CALLED MANNA STRAIGHT after, but she had already turned off her non-personal phone.

It is an hour later. Manna and Eschewal are snuggled up on the couch. The stylish chrome fireplace blows out warm heat; the lights are dimmed low, and the TV plays R&B slow jam videos.

Eschewal's penis is rock hard as it beats against Manna's bottom. She can feel it, and it is turning her on. Her nipples stiffen.

He grips her tighter but does not grind on her. He slips his fingers in between hers and moves his body further onto her.

He sniffs her hair and plants a soft kiss on her head. He sniffs her scent again and feels love seep through. He closes his eyes; a smile crosses his face. An image of him and her married with two children stains his imagination.

He sees his future as similar to his grandparents' life: a beautiful, well-kept house, good food always cooking on the stove, a nice large family car, and a garage.

The idea of working hard to support her and their new family gives him the most excitement.

He drifts off into sleep, feeling that his future is bright for the first time in his life, and nothing can go wrong.

'The black book wasn't right; I didn't have to become a creator of values to receive happiness & riches.'

Von Mozan

These are his last thoughts before he falls into a peaceful sleep with Manna in his arms.

Chapter 69

IT IS THE FOLLOWING day, and Manna kisses Eschewal on the lips, without tongue, and jumps out of the car. She almost skips to her front door. She turns and waves goodbye. Eschewal notices her smile, the type of smile that beams not only from the mouth but from the eyes. That would be the last time he would ever see it again, that great big smile.

She closes the front door, rests her back on it for a while, and feels like screaming with joy. She gets herself together and blows out air, then goes to the bathroom. She pulls out her non-personal phone and turns it on. The phone beeps and then flashes up a message. She listens to it before setting the bath. It is Spiv, and he sounds urgent. She plans to call him back after taking a bath, but before she can get undressed and stick the phone on the charger, the phone rings.

"Hey, what's up, girl?" asks Spiv.

"Hold on," says Manna as she sticks the charger on the phone. "Yeah, nothing much. I'm just about to step in the bath."

"Okay," responds Spiv, "did you get my message?"

"Yeah, what's up?" says Manna as she sits down on her bed and unclips her bra.

"Nah, I just want to ask you something. I was talking with one of my friends, yeah... listen, you know that guy you were telling me about, is he also called Eros?"

She pauses for a second. "Um, why?"

Dirty Dog

"Ter, listen, I found out something yesterday that I think you should know."

"What?"

"I don't know if I should tell you the horror."

"Just tell me, man, go on," she pleads.

"Well, listen, if he's also called Eros, then I heard he ran a battery on your cousin, Salacious."

Horror, distress, and confusion explode within Manna. Her heart seems to sink to her big toe. She does not want to believe it, but deep down, she thinks it might be true.

"Oi, Manna, are you there?"

She regains her voice. "Yeah, yeah, I've got to go. I'll talk to you later."

She has a plan. Her hand trembles as she pushes the send button. Eschewal's name flashes up on her screen.

Chapter 70

ESCHEWAL SPINS ON HIS heels and slides across the floor as if he is performing and singing on stage. He is on his way to meet Manna and surprise her with a romantic night out. He puts the final grooming touch to the sweet-boy standard and steps out the door.

It has only been two days since he has seen her, but it feels like two weeks; he is even happier because she has invited him to her house. Unknowingly, it is a setup. She plans to display a picture of Salacious, and when he arrives, she'll inform him that the girl in the picture is her cousin and best friend. She will then wait to see if he admits to knowing Salacious and how.

Eschewal has arrived at Manna's house. His heart is racing as he waits for the front door to open.

She opens it with a forced smile.

He notices but thinks nothing of it. He bends over and kisses her.

He follows her into the living area.

With the most natural manner, she can manage, she points at Salacious' picture, which is perched atop the TV. "Ah, that's my cousin and best friend, Salacious," she says.

As if fighting a gale-force wind, Eschewal moves towards the picture. As the face comes into view, his legs feel as if they are about to buckle underneath him. His heart gives him the sensation as if it has snapped in two at knowing the only girl that he could ever love at that moment has disappeared from his life.

He regains his composure and looks at Manna to see if she has read his facial expression.

She has her back turned; she does not want it to be confirmed.

As he speaks, shivers run down her spine.

"Oi, Manna…"

She wants to block her hearing.

"Um, listen," he begins, "I've left my phone in the car. I'm just gonna go down and get it, yeah?"

Manna relaxes and then nods.

Eschewal walks out of the room and heads outside; he needs time to think.

Chapter 71

ESCHEWAL PUNCHES THE AIR. He feels as if a heated knife is stuck in his heart. He shakes his head, knowing he has lost her, the only woman he believes he could ever love. He sighs. He was planning to start saving for the next five years, buy Manna a beautiful ring, get down on one knee, and propose marriage.

He closes his eyes and thinks back to the black book. He wonders if his loss of interest in becoming a creator of values after he first saw Manna in the park is why he lost her. He feels it might be. He thinks hard about what the black book would suggest he do in a situation like this. The only thing that comes to mind is: *fully integrated honesty*.

He grits his teeth and heads back up the stairs. He has decided to be fair with Manna and will not continue the relationship with deceit.

He enters the room; he looks into Manna's eyes. The thought crosses his mind to say nothing, but he knows that would only cause his true love long-term pain. He could never do that; he loves her so much already.

It feels like a nightmare as if he is not telling her how he knows the girl in the picture.

Once the last word jumps off his lips, the heartbreak that sweeps over Manna's features is visible.

Three Weeks Later

Chapter 72

AFTER THE SADNESS SWOOPED over Manna's face, Eschewal dreamed he would touch her face again. But she had chosen her friendship with Salacious over a possible happy and loving marriage.

Eschewal had lost the love of his life but learned a deadly lesson: *most people do not want fairness. Manna would have been happy if Eschewal had acted as if he had never seen Salacious before. She would have been glad to be kept ignorant.*

He holds onto the bathroom sink. He looks into the mirror and sees a different face; it is not the face of three weeks ago. The happy face that Manna gave him, the face that finally had something to smile about and laugh. His insides are getting ready to cry, but he will not let himself release tears.

He releases his grip and nods. It is time to let go and move on. A tear almost falls. He asks himself, *'How can I move on without Manna in my life?'*

From the moment he saw her in the park, it was love. Love that feels as if it would never go away. It was true, it was real, and it was powerful. No matter what anybody says, *"That was not love, it was only lust because you cannot love someone that quick. You did not even know her for long enough."*

Nope. Eschewal knew this was not true because he could not control what he felt. What he felt could only be love. What he felt had even made him forget about becoming a creator of values and receiving the

Dirty Dog

happiness & riches the black book had promised.

He shakes his head. He now has to get used to living his life without the love of his life. The corner of his mouth turns down, and he wishes he could have plucked up the courage and told Manna he had spent one year searching for her.

He huffs and leaves the bathroom wondering, *'Would she have even cared, or would it have made a difference?'*

Chapter 73

ESCHEWAL ENTERS HIS LIVING room and plops himself in front of the TV after his dull day at work.

It is a Friday evening, and he is about to settle in for a night filled with reality shows and comedies when his phone rings. He jumps up with his heart pounding, wishing it is Manna. He sucks his teeth as Deuce's name flashes up on the screen.

Deuce hopes he has timed things perfectly. He reckons that by now, Eschewal will have got Manna enough out of his system to become a player again.

Deuce received a call from Spiv moments after Eschewal had told Manna what he had done with her cousin. Spiv went on to be the shoulder for Manna to cry on, and later, he became the main man in her life. Spiv finally had his prize. He had not yet decided what play to take on Manna whether to have sex with her for a few months and then get rid of her, or make her the mother of his child.

Eschewal answers the phone and snaps, "Yeah, mate, what's up?"

"Rah, you sound upset, bruv. What's going on?"

"Nah, man, I'm safe," lies Eschewal, "I'm just tired, man."

"Yeah," Deuce pauses. He wants to laugh but controls himself and continues, "So what, you linking wifey tonight?"

Eschewal feels a lump rise in his throat. "Nah, nah, me and her done, bruv."

Deuce holds back another laugh. "What, already? What happened?"

Eschewal says. "Ter, bruv, you're not gonna believe it, you know the girl invited me to her yard, and the moment I step in the door, she shows me a picture of her cousin. Ter, and guess who the cousin was? The same chick we mashed down in my yard."

Deuce pulls the phone away from his ear and bites his lip so he will not crack up laughing. "What, don't lie. So what happened?"

"I told her, innit. I told her about the threesome."

Deuce's mouth drops. "What, are you nuts? You can't tell girls them things. You can't be honest with girls. Listen, girls expect to be lied to; they love being treated bad. It gives them something to complain about, innit. Look at me and my wifey. I don't stop give her bun, and she don't stop call me a bastard and a dirty dog, but she won't leave me because I won't admit nothing. Come on, bruv, that's the game, gee. Lie and cheat and don't get caught, then it's all good."

Eschewal shakes his head. "Nah, I'm a different yute. I can't live my life like that."

Deuce raises his eyebrows and taps his steering wheel. "Bruv, what's happened to you? You never used to be like this back in the day."

Eschewal thinks about whether he should tell Deuce that reading the black book changed him. He decides not to and lets Deuce continue.

"Come on bruv," begins Deuce, "you should forget about that nice guy shit because all girls think that all guys are bastards and dirty dogs." He licks his lips. "Oi, anyway, forget about her. She weren't meant for you. Listen, if you're on it, I've got a link for tomorrow, you know?"

Eschewal pauses in thought... *'Linking back with Deuce is the last thing I want.'* However, he decides he

Dirty Dog

will because he has concluded that he lost Manna and his chance of happiness & riches because he forgot about becoming a creator of values. He still feels that finding a wife will make him become a creator of values and guarantee his happiness & riches. Therefore, he is sure if he continues to find a new wife and does not forget about becoming a creator of values, happiness & riches will be his forever.

"Yeah, alright, bruv, I'm on it. I'll link you tomorrow." Eschewal ends the call and grips his phone. He smiles. He is ready to hit the road again, but this time, he will not forget about the ultimate goal – becoming a creator of values.

Chapter 74

WHEN ESCHEWAL PICKED DEUCE up from his house, the sun was still in the sky. The winter sun is on its way down, turning day to dusk as Eschewal drives down a road filled with a hundred shops, selling everything from alcohol to gravestones.

Deuce turns down the volume of the music and grips his phone. "Little bitch, little rarse bitches, little jezzys," he says, then looks over at Eschewal. "I'm telling you, you know, bruv, these girls are fools, you know, they're stupid, blood. You get me? It's a good thing I've got this other link lined up."

Eschewal takes his eyes off the road. "So what, are these other links nice then?"

"Yeah, man," lies Deuce. He purposely chose these girls over the other girls because the other girls were too pretty. He could not risk Eschewal falling in love with one of them and leaving him stranded again without a driver to meet all the other girls he plans to meet without his girlfriend's knowledge. "Yeah, they're kinda nice still," He flicks his nose and switches back to talking about the pretty girls that he is pretending rejected his call. "Yeah, but them other bitches, man." He says, lying about the pretty girls. "They've got me mad. Try lock off their phone on, man — little waste-chicks. I swear I'll give them one box in their face if I ever see them. Yeah, I lick that over, star. Make them know that I'm not a rarse idiot. You get me, though, blood?"

Von Mozan

Eschewal nods and keeps on driving. He hopes he will be able to turn this girl into his wife.

Chapter 75

THE TIME IS FIVE minutes to twelve. Eschewal has his girl sitting on his bed. He shakes his head and then looks over at the girl.

He focuses on the best parts of her as if he is analyzing and appraising an exquisite painting. He looks at her hair, which reflects a glowing sheen. *'That is the best part of her,'* he thinks.

He places both legs on his bed and says, "Oi, how come you're sitting way over there? You're not scared of me, are you?"

The girl shakes her head. "No."

"Well, come here then."

She slides over and lays across his lap.

He strokes her straight, silky smooth hair.

She looks up and smiles, revealing short wide-spaced teeth.

He feels this is the worst part of her, but if looked at another way, it makes her look cute. He decides to test the waters. He leans in for a kiss… her mouth tastes fresh. He pulls her buttons and unbuckles her belt. He fights with her jeans until he gets them down.

Eschewal and the girl caress and kiss each other in a romantic embrace. He has his eyes closed, and Manna pops into his mind. He throws the girl over and deep French kisses her while bumping and grinding.

"Mmmm," he says.

The girl grips him behind his neck and says, "Oh, baby, I want you."

Dirty Dog

He responds with kisses up and down her neck, then whispers, "Ah, Manna, I want you too."

The girl moves her neck away from his mouth. "What? What did you call me?"

He opens his eyes and coughs. "Err? Um, nothing, man."

"Oh," she responds, then gives him back her neck.

He kisses her forehead and says, "Nah, you know what? Let's chill for a minute."

"Why, what's wrong?"

"Nah, nothing," he lies as he puts his arms behind his head and thinks, *'I can never fake liking someone. It has to be real.'*

"Hug me, please," says the girl.

With vexation on his face and guilt in his heart, he turns around and hugs the girl while knowing he will never meet her again and she will never know why.

He closes his eyes and drifts off into a dream, wishing he had Manna in his arms.

Chapter 76

ESCHEWAL YAWNS. *I REALLY hate Mondays*, he thinks. He only had four hours' sleep, and now he is sitting in front of his computer screen, wishing his private spaceship would beam him up.

He rubs the corners of his eyes and blinks twice. He feels his brain hurt; the tiredness is killing him from trying to stay awake.

He closes his eyes for a moment and contemplates, *'I might have to put some poisonous caffeine in my blood to keep me awake.'*

As he opens his eyes, in steps a girl, who he thinks is Manna. His heart skips a few beats; he is now fully awake.

The office manager introduces the girl, "Hi, everyone. This is Reasha, the new temp. She'll be with us for a few days, so please make her feel welcome."

The office manager directs Reasha to her desk, two desks behind Eschewal's desk.

It is like falling in love all over again. Reasha wears her hair the same way as Manna, thrown back away from her face revealing a beautiful smile with straight white teeth. Reasha is about the same height as Manna, her shoulder dropping just beneath Eschewal's armpit. She smiles as she steps past.

Eschewal sniffs, and a sweet scent of peaches hits him. He nods and thinks, *'Yeah, lunchtime, I'm gonna make my move.'*

Chapter 77

LUNCHTIME ARRIVES. ESCHEWAL SPENDS most of the morning, wondering what approach to take with Reasha.

He watches as she eats the last of her sandwich and rises from the table.

His palms become sweaty; his heart rate speeds up. His legs go weak, and his mind spins into the world of self-doubt.

'What if she blows me out?' he says to himself. He has decided on the smooth sexy approach with a bit of ruff. *'What if this approach is wrong? Should I go for the respectful-modest approach? Shit, which one should I use?'*

He breathes in and out heavily. *'Damn, be cool fool.'*

Calm and steady, he stands up. He leaves his plate behind and trails Reasha towards the exit.

Unaware, Reasha walks through the swinging doors to the elevators. He follows. As the elevator door opens, he grips her arm. "Excuse me," he says, looking deep into her eyes, "I know you're not gonna keep acting as if you ain't noticed me watching you?"

She smiles and replies, "Yeah, I've noticed, but why didn't you say something to me in the office?"

He releases his grip but keeps hold of her hand, and as he caresses it with soft strokes, he says in a ghetto tone, "You listening, it's true say I don't want people to know my business, you feel me?" He does not wait for a reply as he adds, "Can I get your number?"

Reasha smiles and nods.

Von Mozart
He takes out his phone and punches in the number.

Chapter 78

ESCHEWAL ROLLS OVER ONTO his front and stretches for the phone. He looks at the time. It reads nine thirty pm. He thinks, *'Yeah, the perfect time to call a girl who might be into watching soap operas.'*

He sits up and dials the number… four rings later, it is answered.

"Yeah, hello," he begins, "is this, um, Reasha?" He waits for the reply, then says, "Ah yeah, what's up, babes? It's Eschewal from work. You remember me, yeah?"

Reasha licks her lips and says sweetly, "Of course I do. I only met you today; I'm not that bad."

He laughs then says, "Okay, girl, so what you up to anyway?"

"Oh, I'm just chilling, watching some rubbish on TV."

He smiles, and with charm in his voice, he says, "I'm glad I'm not disturbing you because I wouldn't want to start off on a bad foot."

"No, you're doing just fine," she replies with a giggle.

He begins the get-to-know-you conversation, "So apart from watching TV, what else do you like doing in your spare time?"

"Oh, I like to read and listen to music."

Eschewal jumps on the music reference, which he plans to use as the lead up to the date suggestion. "Okay, what type of music do you like?"

Dirty Dog

"Um, you know, I like a bit of everything."

"Yeah, me too. Do you go out raving a lot?"

Reasha turns the TV onto a music channel and then answers, "Nah, not really. I mostly go to wine bars if I go out."

"Yeah, I prefer going to wine bars myself than raving."

A moment of silence passes. He follows up by getting the answer to the most undesirable qualities he dislikes in a woman. "Do you smoke and drink?"

"No, I don't smoke, but I do drink. Only when I go out, though."

He is happy enough that she only drinks. He can work with that. So he decides to jump straight in with the date suggestion. He invites her to a wine bar at the weekend, where they play live music by chic musical artists.

She accepts the invite with excitement.

He goes over the date details and then ends the call.

Chapter 79

DEUCE SITS IN HIS parked car, two streets away from where Eschewal lives. He has just arranged two meetings with two sets of different girls, and he needs help. He activates Eschewal's number and waits for it to be answered.

Eschewal hears his phone ringing but is in no hurry to answer it as he sees Deuce's name flashing on the screen.

He adds the finishing grooming touches to the sweet-boy standard and replaces the bottle of sweet scent on the table. He rubs the liquid on the side of his face, around his neck, and over his ears. His phone is still ringing. He picks it up, walks towards the front door, and puts Deuce out of his wait. "Yes, blood. What's going on, bruv?"

With agitation in his voice, Deuce answers the question with a question, "How you took so long to answer the phone, blood?"

Eschewal sucks his teeth. "Just cool, man, I'm just about to step out, innit."

"Yeah, where you off to?" Deuce does not wait for Eschewal to answer. "Because you know I have a link for you and me. A big link this time, blood. Trust me, both of these chicks are heavy, criss."

With a smile on his face, Eschewal replies, "Nah, I'm going on a link now, blood."

A jealous rage fires up in Deuce at knowing that Eschewal got himself a date and did not even think to bring him in on the friend. He keeps his anger from exploding and says, "Yeah, true stories. Who's that then, cuz?"

"Some chick that I met at work, she looks alright still."

Deuce's lips turn down into a smirk as he says, "Are you looking to chop it tonight, then?"

Eschewal walks up to his kitchen to check that all fires and electrical points are turned off as he answers, "Boy, I don't even know, blood because I feel say she might be a jezz but an undercover jezz. You know the type, to hold back the sex on the first night." He does not believe his last statement; he only said it to deter Deuce from asking to be brought in on a threesome, but Eschewal has fallen into a trap without knowing.

"Yeah," begins Deuce with cunningness. "She seems long, bruv. You should blow her out and come on my link because it's definite sex we're sexing, and trust me. These tings are criss."

Eschewal swallows hard. He wishes he dared to come out and say, *"Bruv, don't you know I'm not a player anymore. I don't want to have sex with different chicks. Allow me, please, and help me find a wifey."* Instead, he uses his diplomatic tone of voice and says, "Ah, blood, I can't blow her out, cuz, she's waiting on me now, and look how late you rang me with your link. Just cool, man, and put your link on pause for another time."

Deuce nods but is not in agreement. He is getting his sex *fix* tonight before going home to his girlfriend somehow. He grits his teeth and hides his disappointment as he says, "Alright, blood, it's all good. I'll check you tomorrow, yeah… yeah, yeah, peace." He strangles his phone, leans back into the chair, and contemplates.

Chapter 80

*F*IVE HOURS LATER, THE date has ended.

Eschewal has Reasha wearing her sexiest dress, which reveals her tiny waist.

He is happy enough with the physical, and during the five hours they have spent so far, he feels a mental connection with her.

He pulls his car up to his gates and stops behind Reasha's parked vehicle.

He is glad that she drove down to his house for two reasons. He now has the chance to invite her up, and even if she says no, he does not have to drop her home.

He turns off the engine, and the sound of music sucks itself back into the speakers.

He looks over at her. He can tell she does not want the night to end right now, so with confidence, he suggests, "So, do you wanna come up for a while?"

She pauses with her answer.

He chuckles, "For a cup of coffee or something?"

She smiles. "Yeah, I'll come up for a while and chill. Why not."

His heart skips a beat as he feels the overwhelming emotion of *The Dog* breaking out of its cage and arousing his penis.

He pops the car door and steps out.

Watching Reasha out the corner of his eye, he dips his hand into his pocket and pins his erection up into the left corner of his boxers.

Dirty Dog

He closes the door, waits for Reasha to close hers, then leads her to his front door.

Chapter 81

"YEAH, LET ME TAKE your coat," says Eschewal as he pushes open his living room door and invites Reasha to enter.

Her eyes swim around the trendy decorated living space, then she says, "Rah, your place is nice. I like the way it's not crowded with too much furniture."

He removes his eyes from Reasha's juicy backside as it moves with a life of its own and replies, "Oh, thank you." he coughs and pins up the coat. "So, um, would you like a drink?"

"Yes, thank you," she replies.

He smiles. "Okay, I'll be back in a minute." He points. "You can take off your shoes, you know, get comfy, man."

She wrinkles her nose. "Nah, I'm okay."

He nods and leaves the room.

Moments later, he and Reasha are caught up in stimulating conversation, sipping on a soft drink. The conversation ends, and only the sound of the TV remains.

He turns his face to her. His lips move but not to release words; they connect on her beautiful lips. His tongue shoots into her mouth, her tongue shoots back, in and out they go. Both now feeling friskier, they grind on each other.

He stands up and brings her up with him. Kissing and groping, he leads her to the bedroom. He throws her on the bed and climbs on top. He grinds for a moment, or two, then pulls off her right shoe like a Formula One mechanic pulls off a wheel.

She stops him and smiles. "Wait for a second," she whispers. She gets up and removes her left shoe and clothes; she puts her shoes by the doorway and steps back to Eschewal in her underwear.

He grabs her by the waist and pulls her to the bed while spinning over on top of her. He slides his body between her open legs, grips them, and pushes them in the air. Her feet brush past his nose; the scent of her smelly feet turns his stomach.

She pulls his hand towards the front of her panties. He pulls it away, kisses her on the lips, and then sits up. "Listen, babes," he begins, "I think we're moving too fast. I like you a lot, so I wanna take it slow. You get me?"

She does not reply; she feels confused. It is usually her saying those words.

He kisses her again. "I'll be back in a minute," he says and walks to the bathroom.

The Following Weekend

Chapter 82

TWO PHONES RING AT the same time. Deuce picks up one of them, looks at the name flashing on the screen, and rejects the call. He answers the call without looking at the screen on the other phone. He knows who is calling from the ringtone.

"Yeah, what's up, babes?" He does not give his girlfriend a chance to answer as he dives in with, "I was trying to call you back, but I couldn't get through. What's wrong with your phone?"

His girlfriend's nostrils flare in anger. "What do you mean, what's wrong with my phone? Nothing's wrong with my phone. When we talked earlier and got cut off, why couldn't I get back to you?"

He says, "Yeah, babes, I was up in that wine bar chilling with my workmates when you rang, babes."

She remains quiet and wishes she had proof that he was not in the wine bar.

He continues, "I must've lost the reception, innit, so I went outside and got back the reception, then tried to call you back and couldn't get through, babes."

He waits for her to respond. While he waits, his thoughts travel to what really happened.

After drinking a quick drink with his work colleagues, he left with a female one, offering to drop her home. The colleague once gave him oral sex in the stationery cupboard at the last Christmas party.

Without warning, he parked his car on a dark street, and while caressing the girl, he tried to convince her to have

Dirty Dog

sex, but the girl refused because she was on her period. He felt like hitting the steering wheel when she told him. He really wanted to get some sex tonight. Instead, he pulled out his penis, and the Christmas party came flooding back as the girl performed oral sex.

Five minutes in, his phone began ringing before he could get that tingle in his leg that led to it shaking, then discharging in the girl's mouth. He recognized the ring and yelled, "Shit."

The girl pulled away her mouth.

He pleaded for her not to stop as he reached for his phone and rejected the call from his girlfriend. He held the back of the girl's head and pulled it towards his penis while saying, "Come on, finish it."

The girl pulled away and said, "Nah, I think we better stop."

He sucked his teeth and did not argue. He started the car and drove the girl home.

His thoughts are broken by the sound of his girlfriend's reply, "Yeah, whatever, Deuce. There's nothing wrong with my phone." She sucks her teeth. "So anyway, when am I gonna see you?"

He deepens his voice, "I told you tonight, innit? I'm just gonna take care of something and then come around. Stop stressing, man."

She replies with contempt in her voice, "Alright, Deuce. I'll see you later, bye."

He sits back in the chair, looks up at Eschewal's window, and sucks his teeth. He puts his car into reverse, parks three roads away, and then makes his way back to Eschewal's flat.

Chapter 83

𝓤SUALLY, ESCHEWAL WOULD HAVE been more careful at moving the curtain to see who was knocking at his door. But due to his mind being penetrated by thoughts of his second date with Reasha, he cracks the curtain a bit too much. He would have had time to crack it back if only Deuce had taken his eyes away for a split second.

Deuce looks over at Eschewal; his eyes glint with a hunger for raw animal sex. The five-minute taster he received earlier has whetted his appetite; the only problem is he does not have a date.

"So, bruv, you mean to say you're going out with this chick again and couldn't link me with the friend?" asks Deuce with a slight hint of anger.

Deuce's tool of guilt makes Eschewal feel bad, but he shakes it off and decides to be honest.

"Ay, cuz. I'm gonna be real, blood, you see this ting here, I'm looking at her to be my wifey, and you done know if I link you with one of her friends, you're just gonna hit it and run." Eschewal slaps on some of his sweet scent. "Yeah, you get me, then that's gonna be long-term problems for me, cause my ting now is gonna be digging me out asking why I linked her friend with a dirty dog."

Deuce sucks his teeth and barks, "Oi, blood, stop chatting shit, man. Don't watch that. Man's big people, blood. You can't control what I'm gonna do." He gets up from the seat so he can express his point.

Von Mozan

"Yeah, alright then, so what? I link the friend and fuck her, but it doesn't work out. That's not your fault."

Eschewal shakes his head. "Yeah, I know that bro, but you're not listening. I don't want the headache, and let's be real here. You're not linking her intending to hope the link will lead to something because you done got your wifey already, so be real."

Deuce's nostrils flare. He wants to lash out at Eschewal and call him *"Bad mind."*

"Alright, that's real. I ain't got intentions for the link to go anywhere, but forget about that because you know you ain't linked me with nothing, blood." Deuce digs his fingers towards the floor. "Since we've been moving, you ain't given me nothing. You get me?" With desperation in his eyes, he demands, "Give me something, blood, give me something." He wipes the corners of his mouth. He has to get sex tonight to be able to handle the horror of the verbal abuse from his girlfriend.

Eschewal looks at the time; he will be late and needs Deuce out of his house, so he hands over Keneisha's phone number. "Eya, call this ting up," Eschewal decides to add a bit of hype. He lies, "Yeah, bruv, this ting has a fat pussy. Trust me; it's buff. You're gonna enjoy it."

Deuce's eyes widen as he punches the number into his phone. "What, are you sure? Don't try to give me no idiot ting, you know."

Eschewal does not reply.

Deuce presses send.

Chapter 84

KENEISHA LOUNGES IN HER panties and bra with her eyes fixed on her wall-mounted TV as the call comes through. She lets the phone ring while deciding whether to answer a withheld number.

She feels depressed and does not want to talk to anyone, especially someone she may not know. The drug dealer, Godfrey, whom she chose over Eschewal, had told her when they first met that he had a wife and he was not going to leave her. Keneisha had hoped that she could convince him otherwise. After more than a year, she has given up.

The phone stops ringing, then seconds later, it rings again. Keneisha answers, "Yeah, hello," she says while rolling into the S position. Her face shows puzzlement. "Who?"

Deuce repeats, "It's Mark. I met you a couple of months back, and you gave me your number."

She smiles and wonders if it is Godfrey playing games. She acts the fool and plays along. "Where did you meet me?"

Deuce keeps his cool and replies, "I'm sure I met you at a rave somewhere, but I can't remember what rave."

She laughs. "But I hardly ever rave. The last rave I went to was about a year ago, so I don't know where you would have seen me to get my number." She waits for Deuce's reply: she does not get one. "So you say your name is Mark? Are you sure your name is

Dirty Dog

Mark? Do you happen to know a Godfrey?"

"Nah, babes. I don't know a Godfrey." Deuce decides to be blunt with Keneisha. "Look, at the end of the day, I got your number, and it's no biggie to come link me, and if you don't like what you see, then you can blow. So what you saying?"

Keneisha smiles. She feels like going on a mini adventure to relieve some of her depression. "Okay, MARK! Text me your number. Then I'll text you where to meet me."

Deuce licks his lips. "Alright, cool," then ends the call.

Chapter 85

DEUCE LOOKS OVER AT Eschewal with a smile. "Yes, blood, she's gonna text me where to meet her. What is this ting a jezz?"

Eschewal lies; he shrugs and answers, "I don't know, blood. All I know is she loves sex, but loving sex is different from having sex with many men on the same day."

"What, she loves sex? Does she suck hood and that, yeah?"

Eschewal nods and lies again. "Yeah, course, that's standard." He circles his head up and down. "And she can suck it good too," he adds more hype, "Oh shit, she can suck a hood, bruv. She'll make your eyes pop out your head, star."

Deuce becomes light-headed. He feels his body overheating as if standing next to ten firesides. His eyes widen, and a grin spreads across his face revealing a mouth full of teeth. He lives for the build-up before the date. Eschewal knows this and knows Deuce will now leave his house happy and content with the date.

Deuce claps his hands. "Alright, bruv, I'm gonna blow, I'm gonna link up this ting." He extends his fist and hits Eschewal's fist, saying, "You're still fuckrie, though. Don't get it twisted, but it's all good, you see me?"

Eschewal responds with a smile and a jerk of the head, then says, "Just make sure you wrap it up before you slap it up."

"Alright, gee, little more from now." Deuce leaves.

Eschewal slaps on some more sweet scent and then hits the streets for his second date with Reasha.

Chapter 86

THE DATE HAS GONE well. Eschewal took Reasha to a comedy night where they laughed and sipped on drinks. All that laughing had taken away Eschewal's worries.

His worries have now returned. He looks down towards the side of Reasha's face. He smells her hair; it smells good. The clean scent from her clothes catches his nostrils. He closes his eyes and wants to say a prayer, asking for Reasha's feet not to be smelling. He wants to pray that even if they still smell, he will be able to overlook it and fall in love with her.

He opens his eyes.

Reasha turns her face towards him and notices his intense look. "Is everything alright, babes?"

He clears his throat. "Yeah, man, everything is criss. Why?"

She gets off her elbows. "Nah, you look like you're not really here. I mean, like your thoughts are distant. As if you're staring into space. What's on your mind?" She unlocks herself from his embrace and sits up so she can take a better look at his eyes.

"Nah, nothing's on my mind," he lies as he looks away from her gaze. *How can I tell you that I've been stressing all week to find out if your feet still stink?* "Nah, sometimes I zone out and meditate. You get me?"

She nods but feels, for some reason, that there is more to it than just meditating. "I understand. I'm gonna call you my spaceman."

Eschewal laughs.

Reasha gets up from the couch. "I'm just going to the bathroom; I'll be back in a minute."

He swallows hard as he watches her leave the room.

Chapter 87

REASHA CLOSES THE BATHROOM door and moves over to the toilet. She picks up the seat, pulls down her garments, and sits down. She does not know what is going on with Eschewal, but she feels it could be due to the smell of her shoes.

'But I placed them almost out of the room; he could never have smelt them. It must be something else,' she thinks. She bites down on her lip and wonders, *'So why didn't he take me? What game is he playing? Does he have a girl?'*

She closes her eyes and ponders about the game she'll be playing tonight: *the tight jeans game.* This is where she will make Eschewal fight to take off her belt. Every time he gets it undone, she will buckle it back up. After maybe fifteen minutes of this, she will leave it unbuckled and then make him fight with her tight jeans. This is sure to leave him breathless because no matter how hard he tries, those jeans will not come down unless he rips them off or she stands up and takes them off. But she plans to rise off the bed just enough to let the jeans be pulled past her hips, then look Eschewal in the eyes and say, *"STOP. I think I'm coming on my period."*

She smiles and stands up from the toilet. *'Yeah, that will send him crazy,'* she thinks as she pulls up her garments, takes off her shoes, and leaves the bathroom.

Six Weeks Later

Chapter 88

AFTER REASHA LEFT, ESCHEWAL slumped on his couch with his stomach feeling twisted from disappointment. The disappointment then changed into guilt, as he remembers Reasha saying, *"Call me, yeah,"* and him replying, *"Yeah, man, definitely."* He had swallowed the lie while thinking, *'Shit, I drove another nail in the coffin that brands all men as bastards and dirty dogs. If only I had the courage to let her know the deal.'* He shakes his head and slumps further down on his sofa.

During the last six weeks, he has dated three different girls with three various problems that stood in the way of a possible relationship. He nods and thinks, *'It won't work out with any other girl because Manna is meant for me. She's the one who'll make me become a creator of values. I've got to get her back.'*

He jumps up and turns his house upside down to find Salacious' number. He eventually finds it, and as he dials the number, he feels his heart beating a million times a minute.

"Yeah, hello, who's this?" demands Salacious.

Eschewal gathers his thoughts. He stutters, "It's me."

"Who's me?" demands Salacious again.

"Me, man. Eros, don't you remember me?"

There is a moment of silence.

"Yeah, what do you want?" she replies condescendingly.

He swallows his rage as his old ghetto mentality hits him, *'Don't make anyone take liberties, star.'*

He says, "Hold on, do you have to talk to me in that tone?"

"Um, well, no, but you haven't ever called me before, and now, just out of the blue, you're calling."

"Yeah, I know, but you must know why I haven't called before."

She sucks her teeth. "Yeah, I know all about that, so why are you calling me?"

He swallows hard and thinks, *'Should I pour my heart out and tell Salacious that I want her cousin so much that I searched for her for one year? That during that year, my only dream was to find Manna, marry her and love her forever?'* He ponders some more, *'Will she even care or believe me? Will it make a difference?'*

He blows air through his nose, then answers, "Listen, I need to get Manna back into my life. I need you to give me her new number."

There is another moment of silence.

"What, are you serious? Are you dizzy? Are you stupid? She doesn't want to know you. After what you told her. And how can you tell her something that was personal about me, huh?"

Eschewal does not bother answering. He hangs up the phone and sits there, feeling broken.

Three Weeks Later

Chapter 89

ESCHEWAL'S HEART BROKE WHEN Salacious spoke those words. He knew it was true but wished it was not, so he could again see that big smile that had donned Manna's face when he met her at the bus stop.

The traffic up ahead begins moving. Eschewal puts his brand-new car into gear. He squints his eyes, then turns up the beat from a hardcore hip-hop song. Rhythmically, he bops his head, and a feeling of returning to his brief bad boy days filters through him. Back in the day, he directed his ghetto mentality into channels of destruction, and by doing so, boys feared him, and girls loved him. He had respect, but at a price: the price of destruction to his soul and quality of life.

He shakes his head. Initially, he was glad the black book helped him redirect his ghetto mentality into positive channels. But right now, he feels those positive channels lead nowhere except to pain, which he presently feels.

He moves off but is stopped by another set of traffic lights. The feeling of just letting *The Dog* rip loose and give up on finding a wife imbues him. His jaw drops, his eyes become slits, and he speaks to himself, *"I can't go on, bruv. It's all long; I'm gonna go back to being a player."*

He looks to his left, then looks again as his heart races and his palms sweat. He blinks twice as he

Dirty Dog

watches Manna board a bus. The traffic lights let him go. He drives through but allows the bus, which Manna has boarded, to take off.

As he trails the bus, the thought of returning to being a player leaves him. He has a grin and anxiety in his eyes as he wonders how Manna will react when he tells her what is on his mind.

Five stops up the road, and Manna steps off the bus. She crosses the road and waits at another bus stop.

Eschewal finds a nearby side road and parks his car. He jumps out and heads back over to Manna, forgetting that he came out to buy some clothes to relieve his depression.

Chapter 90

HOT FLUSHES SHOOT THROUGH Eschewal as he approaches the bus stop. He takes a deep gulp of air as he calls Manna's name.

She turns her head. Her beautiful eyes connect with his. For a second, he loses his breath. He says, "Hi, how are you doing? Can we talk?"

"Talk about what?" says Manna as she sucks her teeth.

Her rebuttal takes him aback, but he composes himself and says, "Talk about you and me…"

"There's nothing to talk about, just leave me alone," she replies as she looks away from him.

He pauses in thought as he contemplates whether to open his heart and soul and tell her how he had searched for her for a year, and without her, life does not seem worth living. He nods and decides to tell her, not caring who hears. He begins, "Nah, listen, there is something…" but is cut off by a chunky guy sitting two seats away from her.

"Why don't you leave her alone, mate? She doesn't wanna know."

For a second, Eschewal cannot believe his ears; he says, "What...!"

The chunky guy turns up his lips. "You heard the first time, mate. Leave her alone."

"Ter," says Eschewal as he feels that bad boy urge rise in him. He glares at the chunky guy and bites his lip. His eyes turn stone cold. "Who the rarse you think you are talking to?"

The chunky guy replies, "You, innit. What!" and reaches into his bag to take out a weapon.

Eschewal sees this but does not care because the rage now running through him will numb any form of pain. This person has no idea that Eschewal has the strength of ten men and will rip his head off.

Eschewal steps forward and barks, "WHAT...! Do you think you're greasy? You're not greasy!" Thinking, *'How dare this guy get involved with me and my happiness?'*

Manna jumps up. "Nah, don't fight, stop, stop!"

Eschewal looks into her eye. His rage disappears. He backs off and sucks his teeth. He reaches out for her arm. "Can I talk to you, please?"

She pulls her arm away. "No, I can't, please, leave me!"

A bus pulls up. She runs to the open doors.

He watches as she boards, followed by the chunky guy.

The idea of boarding the bus comes and goes. Eschewal is about to cry as he watches the bus take Manna, once again, out of his life.

He holds back the tears, replacing them with a feeling of hate as he wonders, *'Would she even care if I had the chance to break down and cry and tell her I searched for her for a year? Nah,'* he thinks as he plods back to his car, *'she wouldn't have cared. Nobody cares.'*

Chapter 91

AS ESCHEWAL DRIVES FROM his defeat, the sorrow inside him pops and explodes. It is almost unbearable. He can now understand why some people commit suicide. He has feelings about doing something terrible to himself or someone; to release the pain.

He hits the steering wheel, wishing he had gotten on the bus and ripped off that chunky guy's face.

He fights back the tears – he has not cried in years – since the time in the hospital. Before that, he had forgotten how to cry. The harsh streets, which grew him, would not stand for it. There were implicit rules not to show emotion; those rules were for street survival.

He chokes back the tears. *'It's nothing,'* he says to himself. *'Fire bun this. I'm gonna go back to being a player. Fire bun Manna.'*

He turns his car around and heads back towards a wide-hipped, fat-calf girl. He catches her just before she turns the corner. He beeps to get her attention. She stops, and Eschewal jumps out of the car with his chest pushed towards the sky.

The girl has a beautiful face, and her body is in shape. He tells the girl he will call her later, then jumps back into his car and drives off. As he drives, he fights off a deep-seated feeling that maybe he should hold on and still pursue Manna. He shakes his head. *'Nah,'* he saw the hate in her eyes. It was not

Dirty Dog

meant to be.

There goes that feeling again. It has him wondering, *'But was it meant to be? Her and me, me and her, Manna and me?'*

Later On That Evening

Chapter 92

ESCHEWAL STEPS THROUGH HIS front door with three shopping bags. After getting the fat-calf girl's number, he had spent five hundred on clothes. He throws the bags on his bed, walks into his living room, and sits silently. The muscle along his jawline tightens. He shuts his eyes to block out the image of *The Dog*, which he imagines is bearing over him and howling for him to take action to get sex. He opens his eyes and takes out his phone. He dials the fat-calf girl's number.

"Yeah, hello, is this Kaya?"

"Yeah, who's this?"

He clears his throat. "It's the guy you gave your number to about two hours ago."

"Oh, you alright? What are you saying?" replies Kaya.

"You tell me, innit, what's going on?"

She twiddles her hair and sits down on the bus stop bench. Her fantasy floats her away for a minute. She's imagining marrying Eschewal and having his children, then living happily ever after. "Ah, nothing much. I'm just going home," she replies finally.

"Okay, so where's home?"

"Um, I live in south, innit."

"Rah south, yeah, that's my ends. So what do you like doing?"

She crosses her legs. "Um, I like going to the cinema, out for a drink, raving."

"Yeah," he begins as he rubs his chin, "Are you an adventurous person?"

She looks confused. "Yeah, sort of, but it depends on what you mean?"

He pauses for a moment; he knows the following sentence could make or break the conversation. He squints and goes for it. "I don't know, sexually. Like, do you enjoy sex?"

For a moment, there is a slight pause.

"Of course, I enjoy sex. What type of question is that?"

He smiles. "Okay," he begins, "what type of sex do you like? Like, what's your best position?"

She smiles and becomes flushed; it is good that no one else is sitting at the bus stop. With her nipples pricking up, she answers, "Doggie style. I love doggie style."

"Geez, that's my best position too. What else do you like doing? I bet you're a freak?"

"Yeah, sometimes I can be, but I don't give head if that's what you're asking?"

He leans back on his sofa. "You don't give head. Are you serious?"

"Yeah, I have never given head before. I've had it given to me, though."

He knows this is a hint to him; he plays it cool. "So, are you saying you would never give head?"

She swallows hard. "Yeah, maybe on the right person. Do you go down? Be honest."

"Yeah, but only if I had wifey."

This puts a smile on her face.

He continues, "What other freaky things have you done? Have you done anal sex?"

She smiles. She has always wanted to try. "Nah, but I wouldn't say I won't because during sex, sometimes it gets heated, and anything could happen."

Dirty Dog

He raises his eyebrows. "True stories? Do you like riding it?"

"Course."

"Yeah, but can you ride it good? Can you handle it?"

"Of course," she replies.

"Have you ever been picked up while riding it?"

She swallows hard again as she sees herself being picked up in strong arms while being penetrated.

"Nah, never, no one has ever done that."

"For real? Well, I'm gonna see what I can do about that. Trust me. I wish I could come and meet you now."

"Why don't you?"

He sits up, and his heart races. *The Dog* is out of its cage. "For real, where are you?"

She shakes her head. "Nah, forget it… I've never done this before."

He calms his composure. "Do what before?"

She bites her lip; she is feeling incredibly aroused. "You know, getting down on the first night."

"Nah, babes, it's not that type of party. Nothing can't go on unless you want it to go on."

Kaya thinks for a moment; she is only going to go home and be bored, so she decides to meet with Eschewal.

"Alright then, let's meet, but I'm serious. No funny business."

Chapter 93

ESCHEWAL DASHES TO HIS car. His phone rings. He thinks it might be Kaya calling him with a change of mind. His heart feels like it shoots up to his throat as Reasha's name flashes on the screen. He had not heard from her for about two months and assumed she had gotten the message. He shakes his head, wondering what reason he could give her why he has not called since they met last.

He clicks open his car door and answers the call, "Yeah, hello," he says with an even tone.

"Hi stranger," replies Reasha, as if it was just the other day they spoke. "What's up? Why haven't I heard from you?"

He swallows hard and ponders, *'Dare I tell her that because her feet smelt, I never want to link her on a sexual or romantic level again?'* He clears his throat. "Nah, wait there, I'm sure you said you would give me a call, and like, I've been waiting ever since."

She wrinkles her nose. "I don't remember saying that, and even if I did say that, couldn't you call and find out why I hadn't called?"

He opens his car door and says, "Boy, to tell you the truth, because you didn't call, I thought you were giving me a sign that you weren't interested."

She raises her eyebrows and says, "Of course, I'm interested in you." She pauses, then continues, "Are you interested in me?"

He closes his eyes, swings his car door open, and

Von Mozan

then shuts it. *Time to be honest.* He leans on the car roof. "Yeah, man, you're a nice girl, man."

She clears her throat. "Yeah, but?"

"Nah, no buts. You're a nice girl, innit." He opens his car door. "But listen, can we talk about this later because I'm in a rush to get somewhere."

She almost sucks her teeth. "Yeah, okay."

"Alright, I'll call you later."

He ends the call with no intention of ever calling her back, hoping, this time, she gets the message.

He jumps in the car and sucks his teeth, then shakes his head. He thinks, 'Why couldn't I just be honest? People don't want honesty.'

He sticks the key into the ignition and speeds off, hoping that Kaya is still waiting at the bus stop.

Chapter 94

*O*UTSIDE IS STILL LIGHT as Eschewal makes his way to the bus stop where Kaya should still be waiting for him. He weaves his car through the slow moving traffic in a frantic haste.

From out of nowhere, BANG!

Eschewal hits his car into a station wagon.

"SHIT!" He punches the steering wheel as he cannot believe he has crashed his new car.

He pulls the car over to the side of the road while thinking, *'This must be a sign. I can't make The Dog in me win. I have to continue finding a wifey. If by some stroke of luck Kaya is still at the bus stop when I get there, I'll make her my wifey.'*

He gets out and looks toward the sky while he waits for the owner of the station wagon to get out of his car.

"SHIT!" Eschewal says again as he spots Deuce strolling out of a sweetie shop. Eschewal grits his teeth and wishes he could have hidden, but it is too late; Deuce spots him and saunters over.

Deuce waits until Eschewal deals with the station wagon driver but wonders if Eschewal has made it work with Reasha.

"Yes, blood," Deuce hits fists with Eschewal as the station wagon driver walks back to his undented car.

Eschewal nods. "Yeah, wha gwan?"

Deuce shrugs. "Boy, nothing. I ain't seen you for long, though, bruv." Deuce had purposely stopped

Dirty Dog

using Eschewal to drive him around to meet different girls because his girlfriend had become aware of Eschewal's car. But now that Deuce sees Eschewal has a new car, he can now use Eschewal to drive him around again.

Deuce taps Eschewal's car. "You got a new whip then, yeah?"

Eschewal smiles and nods. "Yeah, I bought it last week," he says.

Deuce returns the smile. "Seen, so where were you off to anyway?"

Eschewal does not want to risk Deuce talking him into doing a threesome with Kaya, so he lies, "Boy, nowhere, man. I was just cruising innit, and that dick head banged into me, innit."

"Yeah," Deuce sucks air through his teeth, then with a joyful tone, he says, "give me a chick then."

Eschewal steps back. He thinks of Kaya and wonders if Deuce will sense he is lying. "Boy, I ain't got no links, blood. I ain't got nothing, cuz."

"What happened to that ting last time?"

Memories of Reasha's smelly feet hit Eschewal. "Nah, she was long, blood. You get me?" He sucks his teeth, and before he says the following sentence, he knows he will regret it and blow his chance of making Kaya his wife, but he cannot help himself. "I'm looking for something now, bruv."

With excitement in his voice, Deuce suggests, "Come then, let's go out there now and see if we can pick up some strays."

Eschewal bites his lip and contemplates telling Deuce the truth that Kaya is waiting for him at a bus stop, and he wants to make her his wife. He looks into Deuce's sexfiend eyes and thinks, *'What's the use? He'll never understand. Sorry, Kaya.'*

Eschewal throws his car key in the air and says,

Von Mozan

"Yeah, come we go then."

With his shoulders slightly hunched and his head bowed, Eschewal gets into his car, followed by Deuce, and drives off to one of the high street corners.

Part Three
Three Months Later

Chapter 95

LIKE DÉJA VU, ESCHEWAL sits with Deuce in his car on a corner.

Eschewal looks at his phone. He is expecting a call from a girl he talked to last week. She had promised that she would confirm the date a day ago. He sucks his teeth, puts his phone back into his pocket, and thinks, *'She was not the one. The real girl of my dreams who will make me become a creator of values might walk past the car at any moment.'* This thought helps him put the girl out of his mind and join Deuce, who is looking out for girls he can dupe.

"Rah, shit," says Deuce, "look at them two fit, tings, blood."

"Where? Where?" replies Eschewal as he spins around his head like a chicken.

"Over there, blood." Deuce points at the girls as they cross the main road at the traffic lights.

Eschewal taps Deuce's shoulder. "Come, let's jump out and go after them."

Deuce shakes his head. "Nah, it's long." He wipes the corners of his mouth. "Bruv, you know I'm tired of churpsing girls, tired of linking, bruv. But I can't stop. I don't know what's wrong with me; it's like if I don't fuck a different girl at least once a week, I can't function. That can't be right?" He pauses and looks out the window. "Oi, bruv, you know how many girls I've chopped; young-tings, old-foots, all sorts." He shakes his head. "I need to stop and marry my wifey, man."

Eschewal wrinkles his brow as if deliberating over a complex philosophical question. "Bruv, your problem is this; you have an addiction, and like all addictions, you must make a choice. Is something bigger than promiscuous sex in your life that would make you stop fucking different girls?"

Deuce thinks for a moment. There is nothing, not even the love of his girlfriend.

Eschewal pops his door. "Oi, bruv, come. There are the same two chicks."

Deuce stays motionless for a second. He thinks he will never be able to give up his promiscuity. He pops the door and joins Eschewal and the two sexy girls.

Chapter 96

THE SUN HAS FALLEN. Deuce suggests a stroll in the park. After a half an hour drive, Eschewal pulls up at the park. Everybody steps out of the car without coats because the day's blazing sun has left the night air warm.

Deuce, Eschewal, and the two sexy girls sit on the freshly cut grass. They have been sitting there for almost an hour talking.

Deuce stares up at the stars. He says to himself, *'Flipping hell, once again little more from now I will be banging another chick that I just met and whose name I can't even remember. I need help.'*

He looks over at Eschewal and gives him the signal. Deuce coughs and stands up. "Eh, bruv, I'm gonna see if I can get some drinks. I'll be back in a minute." He looks toward his girl. "Oi, babes, you wanna follow me?"

The girl smiles and rises from the grass. "Okay."

She follows up behind Deuce, leaving Eschewal and his girl on the grass.

Eschewal leans back onto his elbows. He lets out a loud gasp of air as if trying to suppress *The Dog's* barking that wants him to talk the girl into having sex with him right now. He coughs and fights down *The Dog's* temptation. He refocuses on getting to know this girl and maybe making her his wife. "So," he begins, "you don't have a boyfriend, right?"

The girl puts her hand over her mouth and then

Von Mozan

removes it. "Yeah, sort of, but we kind of broke up."

Eschewal's eyes soften. "Yeah, how long were you together?"

"Since school days."

He nods. "Do you still love him?"

She mumbles, "Yeah."

"Wow, that's deep. You know what? You should work it out, man. True love can come more than once, but once you get it, you should hold onto it and never let go."

She nods in agreement and leans back onto her elbows.

As she and Eschewal engage in further conversation, Eschewal's visual picture of him and her possibly living with happiness & riches shatters into a thousand pieces putting him back to square one.

Chapter 97

*O*VER ON THE OTHER side of the park, Deuce sits in a square courtyard with his girl. He dips his hand into his pocket and pulls out a condom.

"What's that? Is that a sweetie?" queries the girl.

He smiles. "Nah, it's not a sweetie, but it can make you feel sweet if you let me use it?"

"Well, if you tell me what it is, I might?"

He looks into her eyes and says, "A condom."

She does not respond.

He says, "Are you gonna make me use it?"

She wrinkles her nose. "What on me?"

"Yeah, obviously, I'm not gonna use it on myself."

She cracks a smile and shrugs. "I don't know. If you want to."

His heart races. *The Dog* is loose; he wants to fight it, but it is no use.

She puts her hand on her hips. "Are we gonna do it right here?"

"Nah, here is too bright. Let's find somewhere else."

Deuce and the girl rise from the courtyard bench.

The wind blows as he bends her over a park bench down by a darkened stream and performs sexual intercourse.

Another Three Months

Chapter 98

ESCHEWAL STILL HAS NOT found a potential wife or had sex for over a year. Every girl he has dated has not worked out, so this has now made him absolutely think, *'These flops must be happening because Manna was definitely the one.'* He bites down on his teeth as the thought hits him again, *'She had to be the one that would make me become a creator of values because when I was with her, I felt I could conquer the world.'*

He shakes his head and wonders, *'Could I become a creator of values without the love of my life? If so, what would be the use without the love of my life to share the happiness & riches with?'*

He sucks his teeth and twists in his chair. He looks at his blank computer screen. He bites his lip and remembers the moment he saw Salacious' picture. The feeling of being alive and happy began to drain from his body, and just like that, Manna was gone.

He blinks his eyes and swallows hard. He springs up from his chair with a smile. He has been waiting for this wretched hour to come for the past four days to shut down his mind from work for 60 hours.

Without saying bye to his colleagues, he almost runs out of his office and hits the warm fresh air. A headache he had before evaporates as he disappears from his place of work.

Chapter 99

STARS ARE IN THE sky, and Eschewal finally reaches home after spending half an hour in traffic. He will not let that get him down as he sits to eat the takeaway he has just purchased.

He leans over to his phone and calls Deuce, who has another date for him. Eschewal's usual optimism that maybe this date is the one is not as bold as it used to be. He secretly hopes Deuce will tell him the dates have canceled.

"Yes, bruv. What, are those links still lined up for later?"

Deuce walks out of his bedroom, leaving his girlfriend on his bed. He talks low, "Yeah, they're lined up, man. Just link me in about an hour. I have to get rid of wifey."

Eschewal bites down on his teeth and fills his mind with positive thoughts. *'Bruv, you never know, this might be the one,'* he muses; then, over a chuckle, he replies, "Alright, my yute."

Deuce ends the call. Earlier, he had arranged what he thinks are two different sets of dates, who are willing to bring a friend for Eschewal. But he now has to decide which date to rain check.

He walks back into his bedroom thinking, *'I wonder which link to blow out? But they're both nice, man. But I think I should blow out Venisha 'cause I've done hit her already. Yeah, I'm gonna blow out Venisha and link Alena, plus Alena has got a cock-off bum.'*

Dirty Dog

He jumps on his bed, not realizing he has an erection.

His girlfriend notices. "I hope that's for me?"

It is not. Deuce is thinking about grabbing hold of Alena's big bottom. He smiles as shivers shoot down his spine. "Of course, it's for you, babes. Come here."

He spins her around and gives her sexual intercourse for ten minutes, feeling this will be enough to keep her satisfied and send her on her way.

Chapter 100

DEUCE HAS JUST CANCELED his date with Venisha. She sits back down, vexed. She had done her nails and hair for the double date with her friend, Deuce and Eschewal. She sucks her teeth, picks up her phone, and dials her friend to let her know her date is canceled.

The phone answers.

"Hi, babes."

"What's up, sweetie?" replies the friend.

"Nothing much, just calling to say my link has flopped."

The friend replies, "Not to worry, babes. I've got backup. Some guy just called me. I met him last weekend; he wants to link a friend and me."

"Really?" replies Venisha.

"Yeah," replies the friend. "So should I call him back and tell him yes?"

Venisha pauses. "Yeah, go on then, um, what's his name anyway? Where did you meet him?"

"Oh, his name's Mark. I met him while standing at a bus stop. He pulled up in a black sports car, and you know I don't usually talk to guys who do that. But he got out of his car and came up to me."

Venisha's stomach sinks. Mark is the name she knows Deuce by, and he drives a black sports car.

"MARK?" says Venisha.

"Yeah, why, do you know him?"

"What does he look like?"

"Well, he's a pretty boy, tonk he's kinda choong still."

Venisha's mouth drops open. "Oh my God, I swear down, he's the same guy we were meant to link today."

The friend covers her mouth, then says, "Don't lie. You're lying."

"I'm not, Alena. What's his number?"

"Hold on," says Alena as she flicks through her other phone. She reads out the number, and it matches. "Bastard," curses Alena. "You see; that's why I hate players, you know."

Venisha coughs. She feels a bit embarrassed that Deuce chose Alena over her. Deep down, Alena is thrilled that Deuce chose her, but girls have to stick together in the end.

Chapter 101

*D*EUCE FEELS OVER-EXCITED. He has got rid of his girlfriend, and the thought of having sex with someone new comes to mind. He can already see himself rolling Alena over and making her holler. A broad grin comes to his face as he finishes creaming his body.

"Yeah," He says as he pats his chest and moves over to his colognes. As he sprays, a weird feeling comes over him. He stops in motion and wonders, *'Did I blow out Venisha too soon?'* He thinks he must be getting soft in his old age because, back in the day, he was ten times as ruthless as he is now.

He would not hesitate to make a girl think he is still coming and have the girl waiting in the pouring rain. He did not care if the girl spent half her day preparing. That did not bother him. At the end of the day, he always thought, there are more girls where that one came from.

He had been one cold-hearted, ruthless player. He had shown no respect to females and got away with it, but now he is about to taste some of his own medicine.

His phone rings.

He answers it, "Yeah, hello," he says with confidence.

Alena licks her lips and then speaks.

Chapter 102

"OH, HI BABES," BEGINS Alena as she looks over at Venisha and rolls her eyes. "Um, you know what? I'm not going to be where I told you to pick me up."

Deuce's heart rate speeds up just a little. However, he relaxes and says, "Yeah, so where do you want me to pick you up?"

"Um," Alena bites down on her lip. "You know where I told you to meet me, yeah… well, I want you to meet me outside the bus station on the main road instead, yeah? Someone will drop my friend and me off, so be there about half-ten."

Deuce wants to suck his teeth because the arrangement was to meet at half-past nine. Now he has to kill an hour. He really hates waiting around once he is ready.

He looks up at the time. It reads seven forty-five, "Yeah, alright," he finally says, "but I thought we said half-nine?"

"Yeah, I know," Alena pulls the phone away from her ear and holds back a laugh, "but I have to sort out something before I come, innit."

"Alright, just make sure you're there, you know, don't let me have to wait around for you."

"Nah, I'll be there, babes, don't worry." She covers her mouth from laughing.

"Alright. Oi, oi, oi, is the friend you bringing nice?"

"Yeah, man, she's nice. Just like me."

He nods. "Alright, later."

Dirty Dog

"Yeah, later," responds Alena as she ends the call and bursts out laughing.

Deuce throws the phone onto his bed and continues getting ready with a feeling of uneasiness.

Chapter 103

ESCHEWAL TAPS HIS STEERING wheel as he and Deuce sit outside the bus station.

"Oi, where's these chicks, bruv, man?"

Deuce looks at his phone; the time reads 11:00 p.m. He feels like hitting the dashboard. He sucks his teeth, then leans back into the seat and grips the phone. "I don't know, man, they're taking the piss."

Eschewal squints. "Wait, are you sure this is the right place they said to meet them?"

"Yeah, man," replies Deuce as he screws his face and looks out the window.

Eschewal leans his head back on the headrest. "Well, I beg you call them then because it don't make sense we sit here like a pair of sitting ducks."

Deuce sucks his teeth and looks out the window. For a few minutes, there is silence between the men.

Eschewal gazes out his window. His thoughts drift to when he saw Manna walk past him in the club. He feels the way it happened: it seemed like magic brought her to him to give him happiness and something to live for finally.

He feels like crying as he remembers how happy Manna made him feel for those brief moments he spent with her. Those moments felt like heaven, far from the hell he grew up in and had to endure.

His chest tightens, his eyes become slits, and he still cannot believe how he lost Manna. He feels like hitting the steering wheel.

Von Mozan

He closes his eyes and thinks, *'I should never have forgotten about becoming a creator of values when I began looking for Manna because I'm sure if I hadn't, I would now have her in my arms and be living a life of happiness & riches.'* He shakes his head.

He feels that happiness is never meant for him. He opens his eyes. *'Nah,'* he thinks, *'I won't make it win. I didn't come this far to lose; I am not turning back. I'll find another princess and become a creator of values, no matter how long it takes.'*

He looks over at Deuce. "What, bruv, aren't you gonna call them?"

Deuce sucks his teeth. "Alright, man," and then dials Alena.

Chapter 104

ALENA JUMPS TO HER phone. She sees Deuce's number and laughs. She had forgotten about Deuce as she and Venisha get ready to go to a wine bar. She grips the phone and looks over at Venisha. "It's that fool. What do you think I should tell him now?"

Venisha shrugs.

Alena grits her teeth.

The phone stops ringing.

For a moment, Alena feels relieved until, seconds later, the phone rings again.

Her eyes widen as she is hit with an idea of what to tell Deuce.

She answers the phone. "Hi, babes, sorry about that. I was on my house phone." She bites her lip and paces the floor.

"Yeah," says Deuce, "so what's going on?"

"Agggh, you know what," she begins while taking a breath, "the person who was meant to drop me to you can't do it again."

Deuce curls his top lip. "So, you weren't gonna call me and tell me this?"

She begins to say something. Deuce talks over her, "Yeah, man, I've been waiting out here like a fool."

"I'm sorry, babes, it's not my fault, and plus, I was trying to get another ride. That's why I haven't called you yet."

"Yeah," he scratches the side of his mouth, "did you get one?"

Dirty Dog

She looks over at Venisha and sticks out her tongue. "No, I couldn't get one."

He almost huffs and puffs. "So, what are you gonna do then?"

"I don't know, like, why don't you come to my house."

He flicks his nose. "Alright, where do you live?"

She widens her mouth and eyes as she gives directions to him. "Well, you see the road you're on, yeah, well drive down it and once you have passed the fourth traffic lights, turn right and drive all the way down that road, yeah. Turn left, then the second right, and then you will see a tall block of flats called Shoot House. I live at number 18."

He grins. "Alright, I'll be there in a hot minute."

Chapter 105

ESCHEWAL SPINS THE CAR off from the kerb and heads for the fourth traffic light.

Deuce points. "Yeah, take this turning on the right."

Eschewal takes the turning and says, "Yeah, what's the next turning?"

Deuce leans back. "Um, I think it's the next left, then the second right, and we should see her block of flats."

Eschewal looks over at Deuce, then back on the road. "Are you sure, bruv?"

"Yeah, man, what's wrong with you? Just drive, man."

Eschewal takes the left. Moments later, he takes the second right in third gear and travels down a long road.

"So where's her yard, blood?"

"Just cool, man. You haven't even got down half of the road yet."

"Yeah, but I can't see no block of flats up ahead. Are you sure this is where she said?"

Deuce sucks his teeth and makes no reply.

Eschewal has almost reached the end of the road without a block of flats in sight. He stops the car. "This is long, man. Look, blood, there's no block of flats. We must be on the wrong road."

Deuce sucks his teeth.

Eschewal swallows hard. "Hey, bruv, I beg you call her again."

Deuce exhales, then calls Alena. Her phone is engaged, and he feels like throwing his phone through the window. He sucks his teeth and says, "The phone's engaged."

Eschewal spins his car around and drives back on himself. He spots a couple walking on the other side of the road. He swerves his vehicle over to them and rolls down his window.

"Excuse me," he says in his most non-threatening voice, "can you tell me where I can find..." He looks at Deuce, "Oi, what's the name of the flats?"

"Shoot House."

Eschewal looks back at the couple, "Yeah, um, Shoot House?"

The couple thinks for a moment. "Yeah, um," says the female, "if you go back the way you came, once you get to the end of the road, turn right, then take the third turning on your left, and you can't miss it."

Eschewal nods. "Thank you." He spins his car around and hits 40 until he gets to the end of the road. He takes the right and drives to the third left, feeling annoyed that Deuce could not even remember simple directions. He takes the corner, and a tall block of flats comes into view. He smiles as he drives his car towards the block.

Chapter 106

ESCHEWAL PARKS THE CAR. "What, call the chick then and let her know we're downstairs."

Deuce shakes his head. "I just called her, man. Her phone is still engaged."

Eschewal nods towards the grey block of flats. "Well, knock her up then."

"You do it, man."

Eschewal fires back, "I don't know her."

"Ter' so what, you're going on like you're afraid of girl. Just tell her you're my friend, innit, and we're downstairs."

Eschewal sucks his teeth. "What's her name and her flat number?"

Deuce wipes the corners of his eyes. "Alena, Flat 18."

Eschewal steps out of the car. He reaches Shoot House and punches in 18.

The intercom rings and a man with a deep, gravel voice answers, "YES, HELLO!"

Eschewal pauses for a second and wonders if he has punched in the wrong number. He looks at the intercom; it reads 18 in large red numbers.

"Um, yeah, is um, Alena there, please?"

"WHAT? WHO?" bellows the voice in an exotic accent.

Eschewal repeats, "Alena, is Alena there, please?"

"WHO, ALENA?"

Before the voice can continue, Eschewal jumps

in with, "Yeah, Arh-leen-na," emphasizing the pronunciation.

"NO, NO. NO LENA HERE!"

"NO, ARH-LEEN-NA!" shouts back Eschewal.

The voice shouts back with annoyance as he is in the middle of watching a porno, and he wants to get back to it, "I SAID NO LENA HERE!"

The man slams the intercom down.

Eschewal feels rage run through him. He calms and tells himself maybe Deuce had misheard the girl, so he calls numbers 28, 38, and 48. All come up fruitless. He walks away from the intercom, cursing under his breath.

Chapter 107

ESCHEWAL OPENS THE CAR door and jumps in.

"What's up, bruv?" says Deuce.

Eschewal feels like laughing, but the vexation does not leave his face. "That wasn't her yard, bruv."

"Are you sure?"

Eschewal nods and huffs. "Of course, I'm sure, man. Some off-key man answered the door, man." He sucks his teeth.

"Ter," Deuce shakes his head and then dials Alena. Her phone is switched off. "Bitch, fucking waste-chick. Try switch off her phone." He looks over at Eschewal. "You see, bruv, what I'm saying about girls? They're bitches. You can't trust these hoes, man. They're probably linking next man; you get me?"

Eschewal makes no reply; all he can think about is the mistake he made in giving up on looking for Manna. He thinks, *'If I hadn't given up, I would have never done the threesome on Salacious and would now be in the arms of Manna. Instead, I'm being poked in the arm by Deuce.'*

Deuce repeats, "Oi, bruv, you get me?"

Eschewal nods.

Deuce looks away and stares out the window. "Yeah, man. That's why man has to have a wifey. You get me? For times like this when bitches play games, and you ain't got no other pussy to call. You can always go home to wifey."

Eschewal feels his bowels twist, sending a sharp

pain to his chest.

The hope of finding a wife and becoming a creator of values is over. It seems as if *The Dog* in him senses this, and he feels the spirit of *The Dog* bolt to attention. He nods, unaware that he's about to have a mental breakdown.

Deuce scrolls to his girlfriend's name and sends a dialing tone. He says, "Yeah, gee, take me home to my wifey."

With emotions balancing on a razor-thin wire, Eschewal sticks the key into the ignition and drives off, knowing he will do something sick tonight.

Chapter 108

THAT SICKNESS FINDS ESCHEWAL standing in a phone box, the type of phone box which is sign-posted with sex for sale.

He shakes his head and says, "Where did it go wrong? All I ever wanted was one woman. I dreamt of one romantic love, then becoming a creator of values and for once in my life experience real happiness."

He feels sick, twisted, and bitter. He has lost control and will now plunge into the dark depths of the world's corrupted soul.

He scans the various types of multicolored cards. His eyes fall on a picture of a young woman who claims she is new to the country and looking for a good time with a well-mannered gentleman. He studies her further: lovely wide hips, round breasts, and a pretty face. He imagines having sex with her. He sees the vision, so he dials her number.

It is engaged.

He waits a while and calls back.

It is still engaged.

He calls back again. Still no luck.

The Dog is loose and out of control.

He scans the other cards.

His eyes drop to the one pushed up into the corner.

He removes the card and unfolds it.

He feels the picture of this woman is better than the one he was going to call. The only difference is it has the words **_BEAUTIFUL T-GIRL_** in bold. He is unaware of what this means.

He reads further: *Pre-op t-girl (34C-24-34) incredibly sexy, with full sensual lips, long smooth legs with a beautiful ass.*

Still unaware of what the term t-girl means, his palms sweat as he dials for the t-girl.

The t-girl answers.

Chapter 109

TO ESCHEWAL, IT FEELS like he is moving in slow motion as he steps up to the intercom bell. He pulls his baseball cap further down his face, takes a quick look at either side of him, and presses the bell.

A voice answers in a seductive tone, "Hello…"

"Yeah, hello, I just spoke to you on the phone."

Errrr, the door is buzzed open. He walks through it with his heart thumping in his chest. Before he can make his way up, a head pops around the corner from atop the stairs.

"Hello, darling, are you here for Flat 14?"

"Yeah, yeah," says Eschewal as he climbs the stairs. He reaches the door; the t-girl's eyebrows raise as if stunned to see a person like Eschewal visiting.

"You here to see me?" asks the t-girl while looking behind Eschewal to see if he has planned to come and do a robbery.

"Yeah, aren't you going to let me in?"

The t-girl creaks open the door. Eyes darting from right to left, the t-girl moves back.

Eschewal almost closes his eyes as he steps into the hallway. As he moves down it, his eyes scan the carpet-decorated walls. He passes weird, expensive-looking paintings. Before he reaches the bedroom, he picks up his image in the gold-plated wall mirror, and for a split second, the image he sees of himself he does not recognize.

Chapter 110

THE T-GIRL CLOSES THE door behind Eschewal and walks over to the bed. The scent of perfume on dirty skin hits him as he follows the t-girl. The smell turns his stomach.

The t-girl curls in S-shapes on the bed and asks, "So, what do you want to do?"

He shrugs.

The t-girl's legs open. The t-girl rubs the groin area. "Like, do you want a massage or sex?"

"Sex..."

"What type of sex do you want, passive?"

He pauses. "What's passive?"

The t-girl's legs cross. "Me, fuck you?"

"What? Nah, nah, nah, me fuck you." his penis stiffens.

The t-girl's lips curl up. "How much money you got?"

He lies, "Eighty, that's all I've got."

"No, that's not enough." The t-girl stands up, "I told you one-fifty."

He fingers the notes. "Ah, come on, all I've got is eighty."

The t-girl thinks for a moment. "You got big cock? Let me see." Then reaches out to touch Eschewal's crotch.

He moves. "Just cool, man. What, you wanna see my hood? It's not that big." He pulls out his penis.

The t-girl's eyes widen. "Oh, big cock..." The t-girl

stands up. "Let's see if it's bigger than mine." The t-girl whips out a huge penis.

Eschewal's eyes almost pop out of their sockets. Now he knows what t-girl means: *a chick with a dick*.

He feels his body become light. A deep sickening sensation runs through him, and like a shot, he bolts out of the flat.

Chapter 111

THE NIGHT-TIME AIR WHIZZES past. As Eschewal runs and his lungs burn, he feels the first effect of his mental breakdown.

When he finally makes it home, he sits on his bed staring at the floor, clenching his fist. The rage which seeps through him, instead of making him feel like he wants to explode, puts his mind into focus. He gets up from his bed, turns on the light, and pulls out a suitcase from under his bed. He opens it and carefully removes the black book from the bottom of the case. He stares at the title:

**HOW TO CREATE YOUR DESTINY
AND FOREVER LIVE LIFE
WITH HAPPINESS & RICHES**

He repeats the title to himself. He then opens the book and reads. He stops on the page that explains the role of volitional conceptual consciousness.

Volitional conceptual consciousness is a tool that helps one create new values. The purpose of creating new values (that provide positive stimulation) is to allow more values to flourish. Those who know how to create new values that provide stimulation run the world. Every need or want is connected to the same essence: stimulation. Whether consuming drugs or having promiscuous sex, the need or want for stimulation drives us all.

Eschewal turns the page and reads this paragraph twice: *Once disconnected from those destructive forces, you will unleash the full power of your volitional conceptual consciousness. This will give you the ability to become a creator of values. Then, automatically, happiness & riches will flow to you.*

He places his hand on the page of the book. His eyes show a hint of enlightenment; he feels he knows why he has not become a creator of values.

He thinks and says to himself, *"It now makes sense. I had to unleash the full power of my volitional conceptual consciousness to become a fully volitional conceptual conscious being. Fully volitional conceptual conscious beings who take action create their destinies and receive true happiness & riches."*

He smiles. He knows becoming a creator of values is not automatic in finding a wife or disconnecting from the destructive forces.

He shakes his head as a more profound understanding hits him. *'I had to disconnect from the destructive forces first, to free my mind to think, then take action and jump from producing values (working a nine to five, etc.) to creating values for others. Then happiness, riches, and romantic love will follow.'*

He smiles once more at realizing he does not have to find romantic love to become a creator of values. *'I was putting the cart before the horse. All I've got to do is take action,'* he thinks.

He looks around his bedroom and ponders, *'What value can I create?'*

He grips the book. An idea comes to him. He takes out his phone and scrolls down to Tek. The same guy he swore he would never phone again. He presses call.

Tek answers.

"Yes, cuz what's going on, Tek?"

"Who's this?" says Tek, sounding confused.

"It's me, man, Eros. What's popping?"

"Ah, Eros. I haven't heard from you for long. What's

going on, gee?"

Eschewal's heart rate speeds up as he tries to control his nerves. "Boy, nothing much, bruv. Oi, you listening? Have you got any moves running?"

Tek raises his eyebrows. "Moves? But I thought you left the road ting long ago?"

"Yeah, I have, but you know how it is; life is hard. I got ber bills."

Tek smirks. "Boy, I ain't really got anything running, still. I only got a little fraud ting running. Nah, forget about that. You wouldn't be interested in that?"

"What, what is it?"

"Boy, it's the import ting, innit."

Eschewal nods and thinks, *'Yeah, that sounds like one of Tek's dodgy moves. Perfect, I'm bound to get caught, and when I do, I'll be locked away from my self-destruction and be able to turn myself into a creator of values.'* His eyes light up as he sees his destiny, him as a value creator. He nods and says, "Yeah, gee, I'm down with that."

Tek ends the call and puts things into action.

Eighteen Days Later

Chapter 112

ESCHEWAL'S EYES SPRING OPEN as the turbulence shakes the plane. He is on his way back from a sunny little island.

The content of his suitcase puts him back to focusing on his mission ahead. If it goes down right, his irrational plan will hopefully wash away his sins and make him become a creator of values.

He looks out of the small plane window, stares at the clouds, and thinks, *'But can I really do this?'*

He closes his eyes. A quote from the poet Johann Wolfgang von Goethe floods his mind. He recites the quote: *"Whatever you can do, or dream you can, begin it. Boldness has genius, power, and magic in it. Begin it now!"*

He opens his eyes and nods. *'I can do it. I'm gonna make my dream come true.'*

He closes back his eyes as the plane ascends over his homeland. One heavy bump and the airport comes into view; he grips the armrest. He looks cool and calm for what is about to happen.

With another bump and a jolt, the plane descends further. He breathes easy as the aircraft touches the ground and rolls along the runway.

Chapter 113

WITH STEADY STEPS, ESCHEWAL walks to the baggage claim. He carries a medium-sized brown bag strapped to his back, filled with everything he will need for his trip.

He reaches the hallway of the baggage claim. It is full of people waiting and dragging off their suitcases onto their trolleys.

He looks up at the monitor hanging from the ceiling, which tells him which carousel has his luggage. He pads over to carousel two, his heart racing a bit too much. He does not know it, but eyes behind walls are watching his every movement.

He reaches the carousel. He stands relaxed, saying to himself, *"It's gonna be all good, bruv. It's all good."*

Forty-five minutes later, Eschewal still stands at carousel two. He spots his suitcase. His heart rate falls, and a smile appears.

He looks around the half-empty hall and spots a few customs officers hovering.

He knows they are there for him.

With relaxed ease, he drags the suitcase from the carousel and plops it on the trolley. He looks left, then right, then makes his way to the airport exit.

Chapter 114

ESCHEWAL CAN NOT SEE, BUT behind him is a swarm of customs officers running towards him. They have been waiting for word from the officers inside the baggage claim hall that the suitcase has been picked up.

Eschewal is three feet away from where people are randomly called for a search. He looks at the officers; they are not looking in his direction. He feels, for the first time, that one of Tek's crimes is going to work, and he will successfully smuggle 27 kilos of cannabis until, from behind, two different hands grip his arms.

A voice says, "Excuse me, sir, is that your suitcase?"

Eschewal smiles. He nods and feels the officer's grip tighten on his arm.

"We have reason to believe that you have in your possession an illegal controlled substance. Please come with us."

Eschewal is led towards the airport holding cells. His thoughts run on what the black book says about subjective crime.

The black book told him: *Anybody who has been sent to prison for a crime that did not involve force, fraud, or coercion is not a criminal.* The black book further stated: *Once the anticivilization collapses, these prisoners will be set free. Or, if they are already set free, their subjective crimes will be cleared from all records.*

This understanding draws a smile across Eschewal's face as he steps out of the airport and up to the cells.

Dirty Dog

He dwells: *'Yeah, the "crime" I've committed is subjective. I've not hurt anybody and not planned to force anybody to hurt themselves with the drug or to commit an objective crime like street robbery to buy the drug.'*

So feeling that his heart is clean, he swaggers into the surprisingly clean cell.

Chapter 115

*E*SCHEWAL HAS BEEN LOCKED in the cell for two hours due to the capture of other individuals smuggling drugs.

He now sits in the interview room, staring at the blank wall. The door opens and two non-threatening officers, stinking of cigarettes and coffee, enter. The taller one is carrying Eschewal's suitcase.

The officers sit down. The one closest to Eschewal presses the record button.

"Interview commencing 15:52. Officer Laurez and Officer Drinkwater. Also, detainee, Mr. Rote, is present."

Officer Drinkwater looks up at Eschewal. "Are you Mr. Eschewal Rote?"

Eschewal nods.

Officer Drinkwater demands, "Please say yes, for the tape recorder."

Eschewal leans forward. "Yes."

Officer Drinkwater continues, "Do the contents of this suitcase belong to you?"

Eschewal leans forward again. "Yes."

"Are you aware it's illegal to smuggle any substance banned by law under the drugs act?"

Eschewal smiles. "No."

Officers Drinkwater and Laurez look puzzled.

Eschewal continues, "I wasn't trying to smuggle it. I was going to declare it. I use cannabis as a healing tea, not a narcotic drug."

The officers smile.

Drinkwater says, "What, all 27 kilos of it?"

Eschewal nods. "Yeah, that's about a six-month supply."

Officer Laurez interjects, "Nah, come on, son. Make it easy on yourself. You look like a good lad; we know someone must've put you up to this. Just give us the name, and you can get off with maybe a suspended sentence."

Eschewal grits his teeth. He has always known that sentencing for cannabis is lenient. If his eyes could talk, they would say to the officers, *'Even if I didn't wanna go to prison, I would never snitch or bow down to the system and beg for forgiveness. You're wasting your time because I must plead not guilty to your arbitrary cannabis laws to ensure I'll be put away for at least 3-5 years.'* He shakes his head. "Nah, as I said, the cannabis is mine. I bought it for personal use. That's all I've got to say, no more comment."

Both officers blow out hot air.

Eschewal closes his eyes and drifts into a state of meditation while Officer Drinkwater recites, "Okay, we have no choice but to charge you with drug importation under the drugs act. This interview is terminated at 16:10."

The officer stops the tape cassette.

Eschewal crosses his fingers as a smile draws across his face.

Chapter 116

THE FOLLOWING DAY IS bright as Eschewal boards the prison bus.

At approximately 08:55, he arrives at the court. At 10:15, he stands in the dock before a fat, jowl, grey-haired Judge.

The Judge tells Eschewal to sit.

The Prosecutor stands up and addresses the Judge. He clears his throat. "Your honor, the case against the people's state versus Mr. Eschewal Rote is hereby charged under the Narcotics and Drugs Act."

The Prosecutor shuffles some papers and continues. "Customs officers apprehended Mr. Rote with 27 kilograms of cannabis in his possession. He claims the drugs were for personal use and denies trying to import drugs."

The Prosecutor sits down.

The Judge puts on his glasses and looks over at Eschewal. "Please stand. I see you have no legal representation; would you like to defend yourself?"

Eschewal nods. "Yes."

As if it pains him or negates his mind, the Judge says, "Okay. Go ahead. Do you plead guilty or not guilty to the charges?"

Eschewal raises his chest. "Not guilty. Because one, I was not smuggling drugs. I was going to declare it. And two, I do not recognize your subjective, arbitrary drug laws. The only law I recognize is universal law, which is: no person, group of individuals or destructive governments may initiate force, the threat of force or fraud against property or any individual."

Eschewal looks over at the Prosecutor, then back at the Judge, and continues. "So, considering that my so-called crime has not breached any universal laws, I am not guilty of any crime, but a man-made agenda driven by subjective law crime."

Eschewal points at the Judge. "Furthermore, the only criminal in this court today is you…."

Eschewal is interrupted by the bang of the Judge's hammer, but he continues over the racket.

"Yes, you're the criminal, you and your cohort politicians who legalize, using fraudulent scientific claims, poisonous addictive drugs such as; sugar and caffeine, which they sanction and seep into almost every food that innocent young children consume. Yes, the moment you and destructive governments disappear is the day everything, which is wrong with this world, will also disappear." He wipes the corners of his mouth.

It seems as if the Judge is about to choke with contempt. He removes his glasses and bangs his hammer of coerced authority even harder.

"I beg your pardon? You're in a court of law governed by legislation, and you shall respect that and throw your mercy upon the court."

The Judge flicks over a few pages.

"I have no choice but to remand you in custody until a court date is set before a jury." The Judge looks over at the court officer. "Take him down."

The court officer grips Eschewal and leads him toward the cells. Eschewal follows with a grin on his face. He knew that with his anti-system speech, which he learned from the black book, the Judge would lock him up immediately.

Eschewal could not risk the Judge giving him bail.

Von Mozan

He had to be locked up now. Right now and flung into ostracism away from his self-destruction and towards happiness.

Chapter 117

AFTER BEING BROUGHT BACK down to the cells, Eschewal is kept behind lock and key for almost three hours. He had to wait until they had enough bodies to fill the prison bus. That day only two people out of 14 made it to bail. The rest will be locked in the same prison with Eschewal, except for one, who had to be brought to a youth prison. The youth almost lost the use of his legs when the Judge put him on remand. It was his first offense. He tried to impress his friends by knocking out a shopkeeper, just for laughs, but now he has found himself up for attempted murder.

As a court officer brings the youth towards the prison bus, a wrinkled-faced court officer lets Eschewal out of his cell and leads him towards the reception desk. Eschewal and the youth cross paths.

Eschewal takes notice of the youth and thinks, *'Look at him, no older than fourteen, shoulders hunched, looking distorted and with eyes showing regret, slowly being lead into the wide jaws of the beast that swallows up the ignorant who fall into the many pitfalls laid by the system.'*

Eschewal reaches the desk. A young-faced court officer hands him his possessions.

Eschewal signs a few papers and is hand-cuffed to a female court officer.

Just before being led away, Eschewal says, "Excuse me, can I get a pencil and some paper, please?"

The court officer raises his eyebrow because people usually ask for a cigarette, so he queries, "What do

Dirty Dog

you want a pencil and paper for? Do you plan to write a letter to God, asking him to get you out of this situation?"

Eschewal does not make a reply.

The court officer huffs and looks under his desk and hands a pencil and some paper to Eschewal.

Eschewal does not say thank you as he is led away to the prison bus.

Chapter 118

*B*Y THE TIME THE prison bus drops off the young boy at the youth prison and travels back 80 miles to where Eschewal and the rest of the prisoners will be held, Eschewal has completed the first part of his novel. He feels he has found his essence, which he hopes will make him into a creator of values and bring him happiness & riches.

The prison bus jerks to a stop. Eschewal looks up and is met with the tall iron prison gates attached to even more towering solid brick pillars.

The prison bus enters the prison walls as torrential rain plummets out of a pitch-black sky. Eschewal shakes his head, knowing he has reached hell and will be here for a while until he makes it to his heaven.

As he steps off the prison bus, he first sees the small iron windows; behind them are cramped cells. Below the windows are lines of rubbish that the inmates have thrown out.

The next thing to hit Eschewal as he walks through the vast corridors is the stink of the place; the stench is almost unbearable. It gets no better when he reaches his cell. Luckily, for this one night and this one night only, he is put in a cell by himself, which means he does not have to endure the body odor from another cellmate.

He sits down on the iron bed, holding his stomach. The food has run out, so he must go to sleep hungry.

He lays flat on the thin, dirty mattress and feels

Von Mozan

the springs beneath dig him in his back. He puts his hands behind his head, and just before closing his eyes, he hears:

BANG! BANG! BANG!

His heart thumps.

BANG! BANG! BANG!

"Oi, next door," says an angry voice.

Eschewal opens his mouth to answer. He pauses when he hears another angry voice, "Yeah, what?"

The other voice replies, "Are you listening?"

"Yeah, go on," says the other.

"Oi, send man a line."

"Send man a line of what, man?"

"Send, man, a burn, innit."

"Man ain't got no burn, man."

"What, how you mean, man, ain't got no burn? Send man a skinny one, man."

"Listen, man, lock off, man; man ain't got no burn. You listening? Get your head down, man. Ride your bang-up, you waste-man."

"How you mean ride my bang-up, you dick head; you better mind I don't bang you up in the showers tomorrow. Oi, don't let me have to weigh you in, ya na. I'll kick your face ugly, blood."

"What? Alright, tomorrow in the showers, you dick head, you waste-man."

Eventually, the whole prison falls quiet. Eschewal stretches out into a sleeping position and closes his eyes. But that night and the 912 nights that follow, he does not dream.

Epilogue
Nine Hunnred & Twevle Nights Later

Chapter 119

THE MORNING PRISON BELL rings long and loud, waking up every sleeping body inside the prison except Eschewal. He has already been up for one hour.

It seems like just yesterday he entered into prison life; fell asleep with a hungry belly and worried about switching back to the old him that got him through the mean streets. As it turned out, prison was not so violent after all. It only became violent for those hooked on drugs, liked to gamble or borrowed things and could not pay back double (double bubble) that was owed. Apart from that, Eschewal realized he could easily survive behind those steel bars without having almost any bother. He did just that; he thanked the black book for cutting him loose from his mysticisms. He had wondered when the purpose of giving up gambling, drugs, and other destructions would have its direct benefit.

He sailed smoothly through the two and half years, reading and writing every day, rain or shine. In the end, he studied the black book to a high level of understanding, read almost the whole prison library, and completed two novels and a screenplay with pencil and paper. He had also got his body into top condition and felt great, but he began to feel genuine happiness every day that he sat down and created a new chapter in his book. It gave him immense stimulation, similar to what he felt when he had

Dirty Dog

Manna in his arms. *'Manna,'* he thinks, *'the one and only girl who can complete my life. That one girl to share and reflect my happiness. If I were given one wish, that one girl would still be Manna.'*

Eschewal is unaware he made a similar wish when he was five years old; this is the first time he and Manna met. It was a hot summer. The local park was full of mothers and children. Eschewal spotted Manna and felt emotions he had never felt before, but it was a simple time before he was abused and became bad. So he ran up to her and played kiss chase. He held onto her hand when it was time for her to go. They both cried.

The mothers said, "Aww ain't that cute," then dried their children's tears.

Eschewal's mother took a picture of him and Manna. Their smiles almost stretched across the picture as Eschewal wrapped his arm over Manna's shoulder.

After, Eschewal's mother wrote on the back of the picture: *Manna, Eschewal's 1st puppy love!* She planned on showing Eschewal the picture once he was grown, but unfortunately, a house fire caused her to lose all her possessions, memories, and a six-month-old daughter.

Chapter 120

ESCHEWAL RAISES HIS HEAD as the noise from the opening of the cell doors comes to him.

CLICK-CLACK! "Morning," CLICK-CLACK! "Morning," the prison officer repeats as he opens each cell door individually.

CLICK, CLACK!

The prison officer reaches Eschewal's cell. "MORNING, ROTE."

Eschewal turns his head. "Alright, guv?"

"Have you packed your kit?"

Eschewal nods.

"Okay, reception is running late, so they won't be ready until after breakfast."

Eschewal nods. "Alright, guv," he says, with a hint of frustration in his voice because he was told that he would leave an hour before breakfast.

CLICK-CLACK! "Morning," continues the prison officer down the landing.

Eschewal's door is pushed open once again. A small man with long shaggy hair pokes his head through. His name is Jest. He enters with a smile and humor in his voice. "Shit, they haven't changed their minds, have they, letting you out?"

Eschewal stretches. "Nah, bruv. Reception is running late, innit. They won't be ready till after breakfast."

Jest moves further into the cell. "Have you had your last breakfast? You better have, just to make sure you don't come back to eat it."

Eschewal dwells for a moment on Jest's *last breakfast* superstition. He shakes his head. Eschewal exposed the destructive matrix of corrupt forces to Jest, but the black book was correct; *some people do not want to be disconnected.* Eschewal learned Jest is one of them and realizes the underlying reason why he does not want to be disconnected. This is because Jest has invested heavily in the destructive matrix of corrupt forces, and there is no turning back for him.

Eschewal is sad to see a potential genius trapped in a mode of thinking that revolves around destruction and death. He stands up. "Nah, these bastards ain't never seeing me again," he says.

Jest nods with conviction. He says, "Right you are, bruv, don't make them ever see you again."

Eschewal gets up from the bed. "Oi, eya, bruv. I saved this for you." He gives Jest his radio, shower slippers, and the black book.

"Thanks, mate. I'm gonna read this," says Jest as he clutches the black book.

Eschewal nods. "Just remember what I've told you, Jest. You're the creator of your destiny."

Jest's eyes light up, similar to that of a child's, but as usual, the exhilaration disappears as Jest remembers his hopeless past and the grey walls surrounding him.

Eschewal's facial expression stiffens as he sees the light extinguish out of Jest. He then smiles, knowing someday the words from the black book will send a spark out of Jest's subconsciousness and give him the ability to disconnect from the destructive matrix of corrupt forces.

Eschewal's surname is hollered.

Jest looks at him. "I guess they're ready for you."

"Yeah." Eschewal picks up his belongings. "Alright, bruv, take care, yeah, and remember, read the book."

Dirty Dog

He embraces Jest, steps out of his cell, and makes his way to the reception.

Chapter 121

THE SUN SHINES BRIGHT, The atmosphere is relaxed. Eschewal has been waiting at the reception desk for five minutes. He is just about to shout to get someone's attention when the reception prison officer appears.

"Mr. Rote?"

Eschewal nods.

The reception prison officer plonks a large plastic bag onto the desk containing a medium-sized bag, some clothes, and shoes.

"Sign these papers." The reception prison officer pushes over three different forms that are supposed to hold Eschewal to three conditions, which, if breached, would send him back to prison.

Eschewal reads through each form. He smirks and signs them, for he knows these conditions will not be able to put him in jeopardy. *Prison will never see me again unless I want it to.* He pushes back the signed forms.

The reception prison officer pushes him through his belongings.

"Nah, keep the clothes and shoes. I want to donate them. Just give me my bag."

The reception prison officer removes the bag and gives it to Eschewal, who puts it over his shoulder and waits for the money he has earned while working in prison. The total has amounted to two thousand. The reception prison officer counts the cash and stuffs it into an envelope.

Eschewal does not say thank you; he puts the money in his bag and heads for the entrance.

Eschewal reaches the staircase; the reception prison officer says in a condescending tone, "Make sure when you come back, you bring a friend."

Eschewal does not reply or turn his head. He represses his rage and walks up the flight of concrete stairs towards his freedom.

As he reaches the top, sadness consumes him as he remembers his childhood. That bright-eyed little boy who told his grandma he wanted to become a doctor. He always knew he had a good heart and felt sick when he did wrong. Every time he went against his nature, it destroyed a piece of his soul. However, he feels now he understands everything for what it was.

He thinks, *'All my beliefs, past actions, before I read the black book; having sex with my auntie, robbing, smoking, doing hard drugs, believing that the black book would bring me effortless riches. And after reading the black book, disconnecting from the destructive matrix of corrupt forces, searching for Manna, falling in love with Manna, and becoming a creator of values, were all connected to one common denominator; the need for stimulation and the hope of receiving happiness.'*

The old man's warm eyes flicker through Eschewal's mind. He smiles as he remembers thinking the black book was magic. *"Nah,"* he says to himself, *"The black book showed me that I'm magic with tremendous potential to create my destiny and achieve what has eluded me for over two decades: real happiness."*

A smirk of enlightenment dons Eschewal's face as his subconscious recalls what the old man was saying while he was staring at the black book's title.

The old man had said, *"This book is the system's greatest threat because it will make you a thinker. They do not want this because if you begin to think, you will begin to see through their evil illusions and their matrix of lies. When you become a thinker, you can solve your problems without using bogus psychologists who do you more harm than good. But the ultimate benefit of thinking is that it allows you to create new values, which will then deliver your reward in the form of happiness, love, and riches. But you must take action. Read as many books as you can – because readers become thinkers, and thinkers become creators of values."*

Eschewal pushes open the tall oak doors, and as the sunlight hits him, he dwells, *'The greatest drug of all; creating values, holds the key to wiping away; poverty, crime, death and sweep in; love, happiness & riches.'*

The door swings shut as Eschewal is sucked into the light.

Printed in Great Britain
by Amazon